Marcia Melissa Bassett Goodwin

Autumn leaves

Marcia Melissa Bassett Goodwin

Autumn leaves

ISBN/EAN: 9783337374747

Printed in Europe, USA, Canada, Australia, Japan

Cover: Foto ©Andreas Hilbeck / pixelio.de

More available books at **www.hansebooks.com**

BY
MRS. M. M. B. GOODWIN.

O, may the Autumn of life grow fair,
With duties done ; faith sealed by prayer ;
May falling leaves be an emblem true
Of the Glory-land, while we keep in view
Plans, purposes, and hopes, that rise
Through all our weakness, to the skies.

ST. LOUIS:
CHRISTIAN PUBLISHING COMPANY,
1880.

These penciled Leaflets are
DEDICATED TO THE MEMORY OF MY LOVED ONES,
Who, though faded from Earth like
AUTUMN LEAVES,
Still live in Memory, crowned with unfading laurels
From the Evergreen Tree
Which overshadows the River of Life.

Drift down, brown leaves, upon their graves,
And lovingly cover the sod ;
Though faded and dying, ye breathe to my soul,
New faith in Heaven and God.

PREFACE.

THIS little volume will scarcely find its way to any homes or hearts save those of friends—friends, it may be, with whom I have held sweet Christian communion, or others, (dear for the words of cheer they've spoken,) into whose faces I have never looked; yet the sympathy of these known and unknown friends —faithful friends, dwelling afar or near—has been a bond and blessing, and with feelings warm and tender, I would bequeath my "Autumn Leaves ' to those that love me, *and to those that I love*, trusting that my humble songs may fall, like a low breathed benediction, upon hearts sad as my own, and prove an inspiration to weary souls to "wait and pray" amid earth's tangled paths:

> " And yield not up their trust,
> For God, our God, is good and just. "

CONTENTS.

AUTUMN LEAVES.

AT THE GATE.

Is THERE room in your hearts, for me, my friends?
   And, is there room in your homes?
Friends unseen—friends a-near, I would
   Clasp your hands in my own!

Have you kept a welcome for me my friends?
   A place for my " Autumn Leaves,"
And for the wayside buds and flowers,
   I found among the sheaves?

For I'm only a toil-worn gleaner, friends;
   Stranger hands must reap the grain
Where'er the harvest's sea of gold
   Stretches across the plain.

The seed that I sowed in spring time, friends,
   In summer withered away
Beneath the scorching heat of pain,
   Bringing no harvest day.

I have little to offer you, my friends;
   Some poppies of scarlet hue,
A spray of blue " forget-me-not".
   Leaves from the sombre yew.

Mayhap, you will find with the leaves, my friends,
  A sheaflet of ripened grain,
Gleaned for you, with trembling hands,
  Amid the falling rain.

My hands, that a-weary have grown, my friends,
  My eyes, that with tears are blind,
Oft vainly search for scattered grains,
  The reapers failed to bind.

Let me clasp your hands in my own, my friends,
  Do not spurn my leaves and flowers,
Gathered for you and bound in love,
  Amid life's darksome hours.

FADED FLOWERS.

I WANDERED forth at early dawn
  And saw a violet blue,
Sleeping beneath its glossy leaves,
  Wet with the glistening dew.
Its perfume filled the morning air
  But ere one little hour
Some careless foot upon it trod—
  It lay a withered flower.

A sun-kissed rose, with dewy lips,
  Lent fragrance to the breeze,
Sighing, with low and gentle breath,
  Among her crimson leaves;
But a wild storm, in sullen wrath,
  Swept over that sweet bower,

And on the grass the fair rose lay
  A broken, withered flower.

From out the depths of gleaming waves,
  A pure white lily grew,
And, wondering, raised her eyes above—
  While paler, still, she grew—
As ruthless tides swept fiercely by,
  Nor stayed their maddening power,
She meekly bowed her head and died,
  A crushed and broken flower.

Life often seems with fragrance rife,
  Flowers blossom round our way,
But sorrow's waves sweep o'er the soul,
  And bright hope fades away;
We weary of earth's toil and strife,
  And of life's gloomy hours,
Where joys are lying cold and dead,
  Like broken withered flowers.

MAMMA'S BABY.

With pattering feet, a-down the path,
  In glee the baby ran,
And creeping 'neath the pasture bar
  His "march of life," began.
At last he paused beside the bridge
  Which spanned the murmuring stream,
And laughed in glee, watching the waves,
  In the bright sunlight gleam.

The mother missed her prattling boy,
　Her heart with fear stood still;
She hastened down the shady lane,
　And 'round the wooded hill;
And then along the dusty road
　Her anxious way she took
To where a rustic bridge was thrown
　Across the meadow brook.

She found him there, her precious child,
　His pockets running o'er
With tortoise eggs and pebbles white,
　While on the sandy shore
His ball, unnoticed rolled away,
　As, grasped in one fat hand,
He gravely held a pearl-lined shell,
　Picked from the glistening sand.

Just then the robin's sweet refrain
　Came from a swaying tree;
With sparkling eyes the baby cried,
　"The robin sings for me!"
The mother caught him in her arms;
　He wondered at her tears,
And whispered, "What makes mamma cry?"
　Ah! childhood has no fears.

LABOR IS LIFE.

The rivulet sings, but works the while,
　As 'tis hastening to the sea,
And scarcely stops to kiss the flowers
　That are blooming on the lea,

The river with its winding sweep,
  Its current brave and strong,
And ocean, bearing merchant fleets,
  Sing labor's ceaseless song.

The tiny shells upon the beach—
  The workmen 'neath the waves
Who build their coral palaces,
  And find in them their graves,
Repeat great Nature's mystic law:
  "Labor alone is life ;"
And he who wars 'gainst heaven's decree
  Must perish in the strife.

THE WAIF.

ONLY a miserable waif,
  A wanderer of the street!
One of the thousand poor,
  That everywhere we meet.

Only an outcast child ;
  So pass him by in scorn,
Nurtured in filth and want,
  Poverty-bred and born.

Ah! coldly turn away;
  Let him starve alone;
He comes to you for bread!
  Give from the streets a stone.

A heathen? Yes, 'tis true!
  And there 's a story old,

B

Of One who came to bring,
  Such wanderers to the fold!

A story strange as true,
  Scarcely remembered now,
By those who proudly cry,
  "I'm holier than thou!"

Ye, in your jewels rare,
  He, in his filth and shame—
"Not his keeper!" one of old,
  Remember, said the same.

"Christ's poor," with souls to save,
  Spite of your steeples tall,
Tempted by hunger—cold—
  What wonder such should fall!

Sermons, 'neath frescoed domes,
  Nor prayer-books clasped in gold,
Can gather straying lambs
  Into the Master's fold.

He bade us "watch and pray,"
  And bind our sheaves with care,
And prune the leafless tree,
  'Till fruit for God it bear.

THE RIVER PATH.

There's a wild, wild path through a tangled wood,
  Close beside a winding river,
And it follows its bendings in and out,
  As the waves roll on forever.

Many are treading this 'wildering path,
  Earthly feet that oft grow weary,
As they follow the river's winding curves,
  'Till the night falls thick and dreary.

There's many a song by the wayside sung;
  Gay songs of joy and of pleasure;
But oft'ner still 'tis a funeral strain,
  With a slow and solemn measure.

On, on, sweep the waves with a ceasless moan,
  And the wanderers pause and listen,
For the low, slow beat of the falling oars,
  Where the waves on the lee shore glisten.

Death's icy hand holds the helm and the oar—
  The keel on the sand is grating—
And the boatman pale calls the sorrow-worn,
  Who have grown a-weary waiting.

Through the mist of tears they can see afar,
  A Star on the head-lands gleaming;
Over tempestuous, surging waves,
  Its radiant light is streaming.

That mystic light is our hope and guide,
  As the boat floats down the river,
'Till we anchor safe on the wond'rous shore,
  In the land of the bright Forever.

MY SHIP.

The sails were set; the breeze was fair;
  Like a white sea bird on the wing,
My ship was launched; I smiling said,
    Rich treasures from the East she'll bring;
      Ah, priceless treasures, soon, for me
      My ship will bring from o'er the sea.

Many a richly freighted boat
  I'd seen go down beneath the main;
Ships with their bright flags waving free,
  Sail forth, never to come again.
      Yet still I dreamed that fate, for me,
      Would send *my* barque across the sea.

A stormy sea, a stormy sky,—
  And all my toil and hope were vain;
The sails were rent by wintry winds,
  My ship was lost upon the main.
      Others have also wept to see,
      Their boats go down upon life's sea!

Ah, when you launch your life-boat, pray
  That all your hopes be true and pure;
Set your white sails for Heavenly coasts,
  The harbor safe, the rest secure;
      A light-house standing on the lee,
      Will guide us o'er life's troubled sea.

OUR TREASURES.

A VACANT crib, up in the chamber,
　A chair by the parlor door,
Tiny mittens—a cap with tassels,
　And the shoes that baby wore.

A flower plucked, by hands now folded,
　Calmly o'er that silent breast.
A picture held with fond embracing,
　Ere he sank to dreamless rest.

A little grave down in the meadow—
　Above it the daisies grow;
And mosses creep around the marble,
　And violets, bending low.

A hope to meet when storms are over,
　A faith that no clouds can chill;
Ah, these are treasures, priceless treasures,
　And we bide the Father's will.

MORNING.

ARISE! for the angel of morning
　Has painted the eastern sky;
Night's shadows have fled to the valleys,
　Or deep in the woodlands lie.
The whip-poor-will hushes his grieving,
　The voice of the night-hawk is still;
Sweet morning, in glorified raiment,
　Walks over the valley and hill.

"Let light be!" Heaven's silence is broken!
　Day's banner is swiftly unfurled,
And the voices of angels are chanting:
　"God's throne is the light of the world."
The hush of a new creation
　Falls over the waking earth,
As the day, down a starry ladder,
　Is sent, child of heavenly birth.

A voice seems to ring through the gloaming:
　"Lo, I am the light and the way!"
Arise then, and "work while the day lasts!"
　You've the promise of only to-day;
Then if thorns in the path crowd the roses,
　And our cross seemeth heavy to bear,
We know the dear Lord, in our weakness,
　Will guard us with tenderest care.

— ———— .

THE PLACE OF PRAYER.

THE church bell chimes the hour for prayer,
　And through the silent street,
And, through the darkness and the storm,
　Wend many willing feet—
And willing souls, O God, to Thee,
To raise the heart and bow the knee.

An aged man—a lonely man—
　Whose friends are in the grave,
Prays for his country, for the land
　His son had died to save:
"O, let the hand which holds the rod,
　Descend in mercy, O my God!"

A mother kneels, and prays 'mid tears:
   " Be thou, O Lord, my shield;
My first-born, and my only son,
   Lies on the battle-field."
No prayer was ever raised in vain;
God soothes all anguish, grief and pain!

A maiden kneels amid the throng,
   In tears—hear Thou her prayer—
For, far away, her lover lies
   With blood-drops in his hair.
Ah, pray for strength, poor weary dove,
All vain the prayer for earthly love.

Another kneels; but from her lips,
   So pale, issues no word;
But to the throne an angel bears
   The prayer, on earth, unheard;
A lost lamb heeds the Master's voice,
And angels 'round the throne rejoice.

GOD IS OUR REFUGE.

God is our refuge, to him we will fly,
When the dark clouds of sorrow are gathering nigh;
When tempests of anguish over us roll,
The love of the Savior brings peace to the soul.

God is our strength, his children he'll guide,
Keep them free from temptation, from envy and pride;
To the careless, the sinful, who stray from the fold,
His care is unceasing, his love is untold.

On mount or in valley, O why should we fear!
Wherever we wander, he always is near;
With garments of glory he covers the land,
And blesses his children with bountiful hand.

His wisdom unbounded, his promises sure,
His mercy unfathomed, " through time shall endure."
Though the earth were removed—time no more to be—
He 's our " City of Refuge," to him we will flee.

THE SEASONS.

WINTER, unwept, has died alone,
And Spring is seated upon Time's throne;
Spring, with her rose-buds, mint and thyme,
Who came, flower-wreathed, from a sunny clime.
The distant trees wear a sunny hue;
The far-off mountains a vail of blue;
The mists of the river, like silver sheen,
Hide meadows fair, in dress of green.
But Spring, with the many gone before,
Is nearing the same, mysterious shore,
Where she'll faint and die by the pearly stream,
While Summer awakes from her long, long dream;
Awakes, and in robes of green and gold,
Whispers of beauty and wealth untold,
Found, where her arrows of light shall gleam,
On meadows fair, by the winding stream;
Of her waving fields of ripening grain,
Her sun-kissed grapes, her grassy plain.
But she, too, faints in the noon-tide hours,
And her grave is made 'mid scarlet flowers,

Strewn 'mid the grass by Autumn's hand,
As she lifts her scepter o'er the land;
Her golden scepter to which men bow,
As she twines a wreath for Labor's brow.
Patient Labor had waited long
For the victor's crown, the victor's song;
But now, his hopes fruition see
In golden field and bending tree.
For *all* there is the Spring of life,
The Summer's heat, and anxious strife—
For Autumn's store of golden grain,
Mortals need never strive in vain—
For those who labor and endure,
The fields are ripe, the harvest sure.

EXTRACTS FROM LIVING ORACLES.

" Glory to God," and " Peace on earth,"
  Proclaimed the Savior's hour of birth;
" God loved the world!" Ah, love divine,
  Nothing can fathom, naught confine,
  And, " with the heavenly hosts above,"
  We'll join to sing His endless love.

" Glory to God, who reigns on high,
  Ruler alone of earth and sky."
  The stars that saw the Savior's birth
  Still preach His peace to all the earth—
" Peace and good will "—this peace may be
  Ours through a vast eternity.

" Our earthly house," by slow decay,
  May fade and pass from earth away;
  But builded in the heavenly lands
" An everlasting mansion " stands,
  Where the pure river's ceaseless flood
" Makes glad the City of our God."

MY CHILDHOOD HOME.

WHERE the mountains rose in distance,
  Was my childhood's happy home;
Where bright waters gently flowing
  Through the dewy meadows roam.

'Neath the pine trees' dusky shadows,
  Where the darkness soonest fell,
Oft my evening song I mingled,
  With the moaning whip-poor-will.

The rose is blooming by the pathway,
  ·The lilac by the open door;
The vine is wreathed across the casement;
  The sunlight dances on the floor.

But scattered are the household idols,
  And memory can alone restore
The scenes I loved, the days so fleeting,
  The friends that I shall see no more.

TWO MEETINGS.

At the altar I saw a fair bride stand,
  With the orange wreath in her hair;
Her eyes were blue as violet-buds,
  Her face like a lily fair.

By her side was one she had vowed to love,
  And she smiled as she gave her hand;
It was joy to know she should walk with him,
  In the path to the heavenly land.

At his low damp grave I saw her stand;
  She was changed, though not by years;
The smile she wore at the altar side
  Death had quenched in blinding tears.

SPEAK LIVING WORDS.

Speak living words to waiting souls,
  Speak words of hope and cheer;
Lift up the spirit bowed with care,
  Wipe away the mourner's tear.

Speak living words! behold thy child,
  Listening with eager mind,
And every thought your lips may speak,
  Will there a lodgment find.

Speak living words; a sinner fails
  The path of life to find—
Point to the way that upward leads;
  Speak words both true and kind.

Speak living words for soon thou'lt lie
  Pale, silent, and unknown;
And living words alone will tell,
  The good that thou hast done.

REMEMBER.

When foes assail, and friends grow cold,
  When clouds are in thy sky;
When Slander with her slimy folds,
  Goes slowly hissing by,
Remember, that the darkest night
  Has the most glorious dawn,
Though tempest clouds may hide the sun,
  It still, undimmed, shines on.

The rock, that rears its rugged head
  Mid ocean's waters deep,
Is all unmoved by surging waves
  That circle at its feet.
The boat that stems the storm at sea,
  When tempests swell and roar,
Will make the harbor safe at last,
  As waves roll toward the shore.

The good and true need never fear,
  Though malice aim her dart;
E'en Envy's arrows, tipped in gall,
  Can never reach the heart.
Falsehood may lead the mind astray
  But it shall die at length,
And Truth shall from the ashes rise,
  A Phœnix in its strength.

THE SPARROWS.

I HEAR on the hawthorn a tangle of tune,
A low dainty carol, to welcome sweet June;
'Tis the song of the sparrows, so   earless and gay,
Praising God with their music through all the bright day.
They flit through the roses, they sing at the door,
They gather the crumbs scattered thick on the floor.

I wonder, if down through the ages of time,
They still hear the words of the Savior sublime!
" Not a sparrow shall fall, save the Father decree,"
He made them and guards them wherever they be.
Surely this is the reason they gather so near—
God watches them ever, and why should they fear?

BABY IS DEAD AND MOTHER IS WEEPING.

"O, father, come home, mother is weeping
    And baby is white and still;
The fire on the hearth has smouldered away,
    The cottage is gloomy and chill.
O, father, dear father, the forest is dreary,
    The night wind is swelling afar,
The face of the moon the storm-clouds are hiding,
    And the light of each glittering star."

Unheeding the voice of his innocent child,
    And thrusting her rudely away,
The drunkard passed on where the wine-cup alluring
    Won votaries to lead them astray.

"Baby is dead and mother is weeping,"
　　Came borne on the breath of the blast;
Unmoved by her pleadings the wine-cup he drained,
　　'Till reeling he went forth at last.

Staggering and stumbling, he hurried along,
　　Then, falling, at length failed to rise,
While the snow flakes seemed striving to cover his sin,
　　From the sight of humanity's eyes.
Golden-haired Alice, watching and waiting,
　　On her bosom quick pillowed his head;
From his slumber the drunkard awoke in the morning,
　　But golden-haired Alice was dead.

Dead, with a smile on her white, marble face,
　　Her death-bed the cold drifting snow—
And there by the side of his sin-martyred child
　　The drunkard recorded a vow:
Henceforth and forever let drink be accursed;
　　I'll ne'er touch the wine-cup again;
By the death of my children my wife's bitter tears,
　　From this hour I will sever the chain.

———

AN OLD OLD STORY.

The bell is solemnly tolling—
　　She is dead, in her seventieth year.
It isn't much of a story,
　　Though may be you'd like to hear
Of one who followed the footsteps
　　Of the Master, we adore,
And laid up in heavenly mansions,
　　Good deeds a wondrous store.

They called her Auntie Prayerful;
  She was ever a faithful friend,
And ever looking heavenward,
  Waiting for life's end.
Many a tear of compassion
  She shed, with those who wept,
And many a wayward wanderer,
  From sin and shame she kept.

"Married?" No, never married!
  'Tis said, in early youth,
Judge Elton's son came wooing,
  And she plighted him her truth;
But the Judge was proud and worldly,
  And issued his decree—
'Ralph should wed a richer maiden,
  Or be sent away to sea!'

Alas for pride and anger!
  The father wept in vain,
When the ship which bore his child away
  Never reached land again.
Lost at sea! Ah! what to him,
  As the years rolled slowly on,
Was all his wealth of gold or lands?
  For them he had lost his son!

They say that Margaret fainted,
  Then rose up pale and still,
Wearing a look of heaven—
  Her dead face wears it still.
How much she prayed and suffered,
  No one but God can know;
Fair as a winter snow-wreath,
  Her sweet face seemed to grow.

Pure, and true, and faithful,
  That was her record here,
Doing the Master's bidding,
  And bringing heaven near,
A martyr's crown of glory,
  Has waited many years,
For her, who lived for others,
  And smiled through blinding tears.

"Why do they sound a solemn dirge
  When a Christian's life is done?
Fitter far were joy-bells, when
  Such victory has been won."

A FABLE.

"Cluck-cluck, cluck-cluck," said the old gray hen,
  Marching along with her chickens ten,
And proud was she as a hen could be—
  For each of the ten wore a satin gown,
And plumes on their heads like a princess' crown,
  And their voices rivaled the birds.

She was calling the chicks to the meadows fair,
  Where fragrance enwrapped the summer air,
When, "Stop, Mrs. Hen," said madam, the Wren, .
"The way your chicks dress is a terrible shame,
  And the neighbors all think that *you* are to blame,
Though I tell them that never can be.

And now I do hope you will take my advice:
  My children wear brown, and are tidy and nice,

And, "Dear Mrs. Hen," said madam, the Wren,
With your well balanced mind, you can't fail to perceive,
That the hearts of your friends with sorrow must grieve,
Gay dress on your children to see!"

While yet she was talking a faint cry was heard,
And the white cat ran off with a little brown bird:
"That's yours, Madam Wren," said the sober gray hen;
Watching other folk's children your own you forget,
And must weep o'er your folly with pain and regret,
When sighing and tears are in vain.

"Your child, though as soberly dressed, as you say,
By that villain, the Cat, has been stolen away;
So you see, Madam Wren, ' said the old mother hen,
"Neither dress, nor condition, our children can shield
From temptations and snares which the crafty can wield,
And to guard them our duty must be."

"And now, my dear madam, I pray you give heed
To advice that I'll give you in this time of need,
'Tis this, Madam Wren," clucked the old mother hen,
" *To mind our own business, is the best thing in life,*
'Twill save our dear children and keep us from strife,
And shield us from sorrow and pain."

"AS THE TWIG IS BENT THE TREE INCLINES."

FARMER, arise! the day's at hand,
Plant the seed and till the land;
Prune the vine, 'twill bud and blow,
And as you train it, so 'twill grow.

Yonder bent and gnarled tree
Begs a helping hand from thee;
Prune the branches drooping low,
As you train them so they'll grow.

Maiden, see yon beauteous flower,
Bent and bruised by the storm-king's power,
Raise it up from the dust below,
As you train it so 'twill grow.

Mother, a blossom far more fair,
Is given to thy watchful care;
Guard well thy treasure here below,
As you train it so 'twill grow.

OUR HERO.

Harry, our pet and darling,
    Was six years old and a day—
He'd always pretend to be working
    At man's work even in play;
Sometimes he was Preacher or Doctor,
    Or Lawyer, or "Lord of the quill;"
Then tiring of these, was a hunter,
    And kitty a *bear*, to kill.

"Harry will be an artist,"
    He whispered it o'er and o'er
That day, sitting beside me
    At play, on the kitchen floor.

So, when he called from the door-way,
  "Hurry, mamma, and see
How I'll take my kitty's photo,"
  I smiled at his winsome glee.

Down through the clover blossoms,
  Down through the fragrant hay,
Where the stately maple's shadow
  Asleep in the sunshine lay;
At length I followed his footsteps,
  Just stopping to pluck a flower,
And question old robin red-breast,
  Foretelling a coming shower.

I paused when I reached the orchard,
  Paused in blank dismay,
For tied to the trunk of a russet,
  Kitty mewed piteously.
And there, on the stump before him,
  Harry 'd placed his father's gun,
And its silver hammer and mountings
  Flashed in the summer sun.

Spell-bound I stood for a moment
  And heard the child repeat:
"Harry 's an *artist*, kitty "—
  His voice was wondrous sweet—
"Kitty, hold still a moment!
  Kitty, hold still I say!
Till I fix this blanket nicely,
  And I'll take you right away."

"Wait, Harry!" I cried, "one moment"—
  Too late, a loud report,

Finished forever the "subject"
　　Of Harry's innocent sport.
Poor kitty, he took her "picture,"
　　Took it in blood that day,
And it cured him of being an artist,
　　Even in childish play.

We made her a grave in the orchard,
　　And kitty was laid to rest;
Red clover blossomed round her,
　　White clover covered her breast.
Harry grew up to manhood—
　　Manhood sturdy and strong—
Loving the pure and the holy,
　　Hating oppression and wrong.

He was first to respond to the war-cry,
　　First to put on the blue,
First to die for his country,
　　With a love both tender and true;
The gun he had used as an artist,
　　He carried until he fell;
It is all we have of our hero,
　　Our hero who sleepeth well.

They buried him under the roses
　　That blush in the summer sun,
Upon the dark-stained battle-fields,
　　Where our victories were won.
A hero the world will call him,
　　And the Nation a tribute pay—
But to me he is "Little Harry,"
　　Six years old and a day.

THE MOTHER'S LAMENT AFTER THE BATTLE.

THERE was only one killed, but that was my son,
   My last on earth, in heaven I have four—
What then shall I live for, when child I have none?
   Laid in the cold grave, I can see him no more.

I taught him his duty—I taught him to pray;
   I gave him to God, to honor and right;
His life, in the beauty of youth's early day,
   Has faded away in the gloom of death's night.

The sword of his father I placed by his side,
   And I bade him return it as pure and as bright
As when he received it, in joy and in pride,
   To battle for home, and for God, and for right.

There was only one killed! how did I live on
   When they told me that one was my boy?
A mother? and childless? 'mid dead hopes, undone,
   Live on! when life has no dreamings of joy?

War's banners are furled, and the cannon is hushed,
   O'er crimson-stained fields Peace folds her wings,
No longer of armies with victory flushed,
   But a funeral song I must sing.

PASSING AWAY.

LIKE a dream our life is passing,
   Like a dream that is almost through;
Like a flower-enblossomed landscape
   That the dark night hides from view.

Like thy waves, O, winding river,
　Murmuring softly, as they glide,
Love's sweet song to the white lily,
　Sleeping on thy silvery tide.

Like a ship upon the ocean,
　With its white sails all unfurled,
We are nearing, ever nearing,
　The shore of the unseen world.

Like a cloud at hush of evening,
　Slowly fading with the day,
We near the gate where Death is watching,
　In the evening cold and gray.

Like the sound of evening vespers,
　Like the hymn at close of day,
Like the dew from morning flowers,
　So from earth we pass away.

————

NOT THERE.

My HOME was very beautiful,
　Beneath the shadowy trees,
Where leaves were gently lifted
　By every passing breeze.
But a cold, dark presence entered
　The home that was so fair,
And stern Death coldly whispered,
　"Thy mother is not there."

Upon the swaying branches
　　The robin built its nest,
And hushed, with low and tender notes,
　　Its young to peaceful rest.
My mother's song, as sweet and clear,
　　Oft filled the evening air,
The birds still sing around my home,
　　But my mother is not there.

The lilies bloom beside the door,
　　And the climbing vines still cling
To the gray and time-worn lattice,
　　Rich with the buds of spring;
My mother trimmed those creeping vines,
　　Watching each bud with care,
They bloom in wild luxuriance still,
　　But my mother is not there.

MAY.

May magically weaves a bright curtain of green,
With flower-buds and blossoms imprisoned between;
The blush of the roses steals over her face,
And she bends like the lily in beauty and grace;
Her violet-eyes shine truthful and clear,
And the breath of her song is the spirit of prayer.

MY CASTLE IN THE AIR.

In days long past, when life was new,
And Hope her mantle o'er me threw,
I built a castle, grand and fair,
A wondrous castle in the air.

There were smooth green lawns and woody dell,
And fountains where bright waters fell,
And flowers whose rich perfume arose,
Like incense, at the twilight's close.

The waves of ocean washed the strand,
Pale moonbeams fell on silvery sand,
The cooing dove sought the shady bowers,
And wild bees hummed in the heart's flowers.

The winding stairs were of marble white,
And glistened fair in the lambent light,
The windows were shaded with fairest lace,
And mirrors reflected no care-worn face.

The walls were hung with pictures rare,
And grace and beauty alone were there—
Music sent forth its soothing power,
And gladness filled each passing hour.

Troops of children, fair and gay,
Made sweet the hours of cloudless day,
Watching the blue-bird build her nest,
Or the tiny wren with speckled vest;

Chasing the butterflies, gold and green,
Brilliant and clear as rainbow-sheen,

Singing anon, such a wondrous strain,
That the mocking-bird echoed it back again.
In such a castle we all may dwell,
If this lesson we practice well:
" *Of the morrow to borrow no anxious care!* "
Make the present joy your castle in air.

BELIEVEST THOU?

BELIEVEST thou? Lord I believe
  That at the temple's gate
Thou'lt surely meet the trusting souls,
  Who on thy service wait.

Believest thou? Lord I believe
  In emblematic grave
Thou'lt meet the soul that trusts in Thee,
  To guard and bless and save.

Believest thou? Lord I believe
  That when we humbly pray
Thou'lt keep us safely in thy care,
  Along life's thorny way.

Believest thou? Lord I believe
  When darkness draweth nigh
Thou'lt hold us in thy loving arms,
  'Till storms and clouds pass by.

Believest thou? Lord I believe
  That we must all become
As little children, if we hope
  To reach the heavenly home.

WINTER.

THE brook by the stern old King's device,
Has been set in jeweled band of ice,
In garments of white the brambles stand
Like gem-decked bride from fairy land.

Ah! the winter's snow and the winter's cold,
Will give back blessings a thousand fold;
So, in many a heart, all hidden, lies
A thought that anon will reach the skies.

Who wealth of knowledge would make his goal,
Who would write his name on the lofty scroll
Unfolded by Truth, as she leads the way
Where the clouds of mist'ry are rolled away,

Must write on his banner: Upward still,
Though winds blow fair or winds blow ill!
And upward and onward day by day,
With resolute will must take his way

With dauntless purpose and will of steel,
And heart that the wrongs of the world can feel,
Like the Jews who fled from Egypt's night,
Must be led by the cloud and pillar of light.

All labor is gladness, all study joy,
And the gold of thought is without alloy,
And happy the soul that can wander long
In the realms of thought and the realms of song.

Life is a journey, and storms abound,
But after the tempest sweet peace is found;
Life is a journey, and clouds must rise,
But our rest will be sweet in Paradise.

THE YEAR'S FAREWELL.

Autumn has lost her sunny smile,
  Her brow is wet with tears,
Her sandaled feet follow the path,
  Of the departed years.
Though robed right royally she came
  In purple and in gold,
Her faded garments, old and brown,
  Are torn in every fold.

With beautiful, gift-laden hands,
  She knocked at Nature's door,
Scattering her treasures far and wide—
  She's dying old and poor.
The wild wind sweeps her vacant halls,
  Her purple grapes are pressed,   .
Her harvest-moon, in splendor mild,
  Has faded in the west.

And while she shuts Time's iron gate,
  With fingers cold and chill,
She sees, through tears, King Winter set
  His watch-fires on the hill.
Disrobed and pale she falls asleep,
  Folded to Earth's cold breast,
The seal of silence on her lips,
  Eternal is her rest.

*   *   *   *

For some the Spring of life is past,
  For some Summer is o'er—
While others gathering harvest-sheaves,
  Find winter at the door.

But Winter's cold, white mystery
    Will break in loving tears,
When we have climbed where angels stand,
    Above life's stormy years.

And if our ladder's golden rounds
    Are prayers and generous deeds,
If never faltering we have tried
    To help the world's great needs:
If, clambering up the mountain side,
    Our guide the Morning Star—
We've battled in Truth's sacred ranks
    We'll find the "Gates ajar."

Though with our gleanings tares are found,
    Or thorns, or withered leaves,
God will accept our toil-won grain,
    From out the tear stained sheaves:
And though chill fingers spread the pall,
    If love and faith unite,
A harvest-home our coming waits,
    Upon the plains of light.

THE CHRISTIAN'S WORK.

Oh, is it not a holy task
    To cheer a saddened heart,
When loving word, or look, or smile,
    May cause joy-buds to start?

Oh, is it not a blessed thing
  To clasp the trembling hand,
And whisper of the higher strength,
  Which comes at Faith's command?

'Tis often but a little thing,
  The cooling draught to give,
But it may yield some fainting heart
  The strength to love and live.

A simple song, a tender tone,
  Have oft such power to cheer,
That weary feet will heavenward climb,
  That else had stumbled here.

We may not pluck the orange blooms
  To deck the happy bride,
But we can strew our rose-buds fair
  O'er the little child that died.

Though we may never gather pearls
  Where ocean's treasures glow,
Still we can guide the little ones
  "Where living waters flow."

It may be but a little thing
  To give "only a tear" —
Or in our prayers to speak a name
  That angel watchers hear.

What if our mite be small indeed,
  Our lamp give little light,
Some sadder soul we still may bless,
  And cheer through storm and night.

AUTUMN LEAVES.

We can not guide the freighted ship
   Amid the breakers white,
But we can build the beacon fires
   Upon some rocky height.

Too weak to stand amid the strong
   When the trumpet calls to war,
We still can pray for victory,
   And the reign of Bethlehem's Star.

And, reaching forth the hand of help
   To the lowly and the poor,
Can guide the feet that else would stray
   Where Sin keeps open door.

As pilgrims to the shrine of Truth,
   We bring our gifts of love,
And thus life's lessons, sad and dark,
   Will prove like Noah's dove.

The messenger to guide our ark
   To mountain heights of rest,
Where, far above the floods of woe,
   Stands *our Ararat* the blest.

AN EDITOR'S WASTE-BASKET.

A NICE little basket sits under the table—
   A grave for bright hopes and dark fears—
As deep as the ocean, as cold as its bosom,
   Hiding heart-pangs and longings and tears.

Sense that is shipwrecked and words that are wasted,
   In its cavernous darkness and gloom,
Find silence forever, without resurrection,
   In the editor's basket—their tomb.

Alas, I remember that terrible basket!
   Its depths are unfathomed, unknown,
There fancies lie fading, like leaves in December,
   Budding life-dreams forever unblown;
An editor's welcome! ah, keep me and save me
   From seeing his frown or his sneer;
'Tis enough that my brain-child, my loved, and my lost one,
   Was buried unblest by a tear.

THE CHOICE.

"Which shall it be, dear mother?
   To which home shall I go?
The grand old castle beside the sea,
   Or the little brown cot below?"

"Which shall it be, dear mother?
   A plain white muslin gown,
Or the richest and rarest of lace and silk
   To be found in Insleytown?"

"Which shall it be, dear mother?
   A tiny plain gold ring,
Or wealth of gems and diamonds rare,
   That would ransom a captive king?"

" My child, your heart must answer
  The question your lips have asked,
Lest sowing in pride you sorrow,
  When the harvest is overpast.

Choose with your heart, my darling;
  Let pride be swept away;
Flowers are fairer than jewels,
  Gather them while you may.

Often glittering diamonds
  Conceal but an aching brow,
And the chill heart's bitter throbbings,
  Bear record to falsehood's vow.

Truth is the brightest jewel
  That womanhood can wear,
Never a silken robe can cure
  A heart grown sick with care.

This world is not all sunshine,
  There's many a stormy day,
And love is the sweetest shelter,
  When clouds obscure the way.

So choose from your heart, my daughter,
  Remember, this life of ours
Must have some thorns and briers
  Among its fairest flowers.

But thorns, and tears, and darkness,
  Matter not, so love is true;
While you climb, keep step together,
  With the higher life in view,

SONG OF SPRING.

TALK not to me of Winter's joys,
  Away with his icy breath;
Binding the streams in crystal chains,
  Chilling the flowers in death!

Give me the gentle breeze that blows
  From sunny southern isles,
Kissing the maple, waking the rose,
  Decking the earth in smiles.

Child of the sun! beauteous spring!
  I greet thee once again!
For I hear the ring-dove's cooing notes,
  The blue-bird's sweet refrain.

"THE MASTER CALLETH FOR THEE."

SINNERS, straying far from home,
Listen, and no longer roam;
Cease all sinning, cease all grieving,
Jesus calls, O, come believing!

Mourner, sad and broken hearted,
From thy loved ones art thou parted?
List, a voice to thee is crying:
" 'Look aloft!' and cease all sighing."

Have you faith? then never falter,
Lay your heart upon God's alter;
For, however weary weeping,
Jesus holds thee in His keeping.

See! the heavy cross is glorious,
Since the bleeding Christ, victorious,
Conquered doubt, and sin, and sorrow,
Lifting clouds from Death's to-morrow.

UNANSWERED PRAYERS.

Does your heart grow sad, as the sunlight
    Gilds the brow of new-born day—
So sad o'er days you've wasted,
    That you scarcely dare to pray?

And the prayers the Father answered,
    And those he refused to hear?
Which proved his love-most clearly?
    Which brought His presence near?

Were you always wise in your asking?
    Does no curse of a granted prayer
Fall on your breast like a shadow
    To darken the sunlight there?   .

And the prayers that were left unanswered,
    Do you see where your wishes led?
Through valleys of doubt and darkness—
    Such wild-crags overhead?

'Tis well, if in prayers unanswered
    We can see the Father's love—
Or feel that each unasked blessing
    Descends from God above.

That in mercy He bids our angel
　　Bear the words of our prayers away
To the caves, where dark oblivion,
　　Holds ever a silent sway.

Ah, *we* can not see the wisdom
　　That sends us tears and pain,
Instead of the earthly blessings,
　　Our prayers so boldly claim.

Shall we cease to pray, since, darkly,
　　We grope 'mid tangled ways?
A promise is only given
　　To the soul that humbly prays.

One prayer is sure of answer:
　　"Thy will, O Lord, be done!"
But this prayer is never whispered
　　'Till victory has been won.

THE BEAUTIFUL GATE.

　　You may enter in:
O, why thus wait?
Standing beside the beautiful gate,
Time passes fast and the hour is late.

　　You may enter in:
The daylight's past,
The night comes on in storm and blast;
Dark clouds are hurrying swiftly past.

You may enter in:
You need not fear!
The way you have come may be dark and drear,
The darkness can never enter here!

You may enter in:
O, why thus doubt?
God will never keep his children out,
On the fierce wild waves to be tossed about.

You may enter in:
There is no care,
Sorrow, or sin, in that land so fair;
Love and peace dwell only there!

You may enter in:
O, who can tell
What joy with the Father thus to dwell;
The "Father who doeth all things well."

MY VISION.

I saw an angel floating earthward,
    In her robes of dazzling light;
Shall I tell the glorious visions
    She unfolded to my sight?

Heaven's gates were like transparent crystal,
    And songs too sweet for mortal ear
Echoed through the mists of midnight,
    Echoed through each rolling sphere!

"Our God is just"—the glorious anthem
   Floated earthward from the sky;
"Then why," I whispered, "all earth's sorrow,
   Angel of Mercy, tell me why?"

Mercy, turning, gazed upon me,
   Rapture and Faith were in her eye,
Though mortals weep, in darkness groping,
   Heaven's joys await them by-and-by."

While Mercy spoke, one stood beside me,
   A child of earth to heaven dear,
"'Tis well," he said, "the Father loves us,
   For lo, He sends His angels here!"

"O, listen, Mercy, we are waiting
   To hear the Master's welcome, "come!"
Thorns and darkness hedge our pathway,
   Above are flowers, light and home."

Then, Mercy answered, "you are strangers,
   Wandering now in stranger lands,
But where the Savior waits to greet you,
   Love binds all hearts with golden bands.

"Stranger and friendless," are not spoken
   Of those who've crossed the darksome tide,
The chains of sin and pain are broken,
   Before you reach the further side.

There, pure and undefiled, you'll wander,
   Temptation free along the shore;
Of that bright river from whose fountain
   Your thirst is quenched forever more.

PRAISE.

PRAISE God, though darkest clouds
  Around thy pathway hover,
A silver lining bright and fair,
  You may at last discover.

What though the stars are hid from view?
  They shine as bright as ever;
God's love, though we may fear and doubt,
  In sorrow fails us never.

No earthly love, or earthly hope,
  Can light Death's lonely hour;
Praise God who o'er the gloomy grave
  Hath everlasting power.

———

OVER THE RIVER.

OVER the river:
Dear friends are there,
Dwellers in Eden-land so fair,
Free from sorrow, pain, and care;
Do they ever think of the earth-worn band,
Striving to gain the beautiful land,
While their feet sink deep in the mire and sand,
    Down by the river?
    Over the river:
While they are walking the streets of gold
Do they think of the wanderers from the fold,
Whose faith is weak, whose hearts are cold?

Do they know how long we must watch and wait
Ere the bridegroom opens the pearly gate?
And wonder why he comes so late!
     Over the river.

     Death's dark River,
     Its waters deep,
Will bear me safe to my dreamless sleep,
For angel watchers a vigil keep.
Then O, my soul, why should I fear,
Though the surging waves I can almost hear,
When Bethlehem's Star is shining clear,
     Over the river?

     Beyond the River,
There's no dark night!
When, O, soul, wilt thou take thy flight,
To dwell in the home of life and light,
     Over the river?

DESTINY.

THROUGH all the course of time,
   Weariness, want and woe,
Trudging beside the carriage of wealth,
   Over the broad earth go.

While slowly, and sadly, side by side,
   Idleness, sorrow and sin
Walk by the door of plenty and pride—
   By the door, but enter not in.

Day by day, since time began,
  Passion severs the chain,
Whose golden links bind loving hearts,
  And broken they ever remain.

Through all the course of time,
  Friends are called to sever,
Some will meet ere the morn is o'er,
  Some part, and part forever.

Ever, as time goes on,
  New souls are born to earth,
Souls that must enter the valley of death,
  To reach the heavenly birth.

"AT SPES NON FRACTA."

THE snow-flakes fell from a cloud-veiled sky,
And Winter, in ermined robes, passed by;
His steed was the wind, with icy breath,
His chariot wheels were the wheels of death,
  Crushing out life and beauty.

The flowers of the forest drooped and died,
Lilies and violets, side by side,
Slept underneath the snow-covered ground,
And the rivulet ceased its murmuring soun l,
  Its babblings of Nature's duty.

The wind-tossed trees with their barren limbs,
Seem beating time to funeral hymns,

And the white earth looks, in moonlight pale,
Like maiden, wrapped in her bridal veil,
    Dead, at the marriage altar.

Death unto life; and life unto death;
Rest of the grave, after fleeting breath;
Life unto death; and death unto life;
The rest of Heaven, after anxious strife—
    Then, mortal, wherefore falter?

Or wherefore weep for thy treasure-trove,
Lost in the depths of boundless love,
Buried, mayhap, on the battle plain,
Unknown—mid thousands of heroes slain—
    His place of dreamless sleeping.

Unknown to thee! but the Father's eye
Marketh the place where His children lie;
As Spring but follows the Winter's strife,
The Christian's death brings a purer life,
    God's morn, after night's weeping.

LABOR WHILE YOU MAY.

SHORT the time for labor, do not idly wait
Outside the vineyard, standing at the gate;
List, the Master calls you, labor while you may,
Ere the evening shadows gather round your way.

Short the time for labor, let no darksome shade,
From the love of pleasure, on the soul be made;
Leave the shadowed woodland, where dark phantoms hide,
Haste thee to the flower-land on the other side.

Short the time for labor; from the sheltering bay
On the tidal-wave, your ship will sail away;
Trim the sails—if need be, take the guiding helm,
Shun the rocky head-land, ere cold waves o'erwhelm.

Short the time for labor; in the self-same way,
Purposes are moulded, as potters mould their clay;
Watch the wheel, slow turning, guiding it at will,
Lest the clay be wasted, tle dish be fashioned ill.

Short the time for labor; see, across the plain
Where the seed was planted, bends the ripened grain;
Hear the earnest workers sing amid the sheaves:
Would *you* bear the Master only withered leaves?

Short the time for labor; summer fades and dies,
Mists and snows of winter drift adown the skies;
Wherefore, dost thou linger 'till the midnight bell,
With slow solemn tolling, life's last hour shall tell?

Short the time for labor; endless years for rest;
See, the sun is sinking in the cloud-lined west;
Don *Truth's* shining armor, work in faith and love,
Only prayer and labor can win the home above.

———

"ORA ET LABORA."

LABOR, Christian! earth is groaning
  With sin, and want, and cruel pain,
While many souls, in midnight darkness,
  Hug to their hearts Doubt's bitter chain.

AUTUMN LEAVES.

Labor! hearts led by temptation
  Walk swift along the downward way;
Gather up the "Lambs of Jesus,"
  Lest in the wilderness they stray.

Christian, pray! Let thy petition
  Like sweet incense reach the throne,
While the waiting, listening angels,
  Bending low, shall catch the tone.

"Labor and pray!" this is the mission—
  The birth-right we all may share,
And thus become of life eternal,
  With Christ, an equal heavenly heir.

THE LITTLE ONE'S PRAYER.

'Twas only a wayside cottage,
  But the firelight, cheery and red,
Fell soft on the white-robed figure
  Of a child, by the trundle-bed:
"God *bress* my mamma and papa!"
  Then she paused in her evening prayer,
And added, with faith undoubting,
  "And kitty *aseep* in the chair."

The night-winds were wildly raging,
  Piling high the pillars of snow,
Though wandering in storm and darkness,
  In my heart was a summer glow.

The faith of the child had cheered me,
   Doubt folded his ebon-hued wing
As I cried, "O, loving Savior,
   A child, to Thy cross I cling."

Their march, the stars have been keeping
   Long years, since that lone winter night,
But memory still holds a picture
   Of the ruddy, shimmering light
Sent out from the burning faggot,
   And the little one's evening prayer;
"God *bress* my mamma and papa,
   And kitty *ascep* in the chair."

Tossed mid the roar of the breakers,
   Wind-driven by tempest-clouds wild,
I hear not the storm-wraith wailing,
   For, soft steals the voice of a child
Adown life's mystical pathway;
   Once again that prayer I can hear,
And doubts from my heart are banished,
   And the star of my faith shines clear.

THANKSGIVING.

O, GOD, our Father! we would bring
   The incense of our praise,
For mercies past, mercies to come—
   O, keep us in Thy ways!

Teach us to do Thy holy will,
   And bear our humble part,
In lifting up some fallen one,
   Soothing some broken heart.

Jesus, thy life, we fain would make
    A pattern for our own;
Thanksgiving, freely do we bring,
    That *Thou* the way hast shown.

Our hands in pity, care, and love
    Extend at Thy command,
To help the sad and erring ones,
    Wandering on every hand.

We thank Thee for Thy mercies, God,
    Thy long-enduring love;
We thank Thee for the Book of books,
    The guide to heaven above.

Father, accept this humble song,
    Which from our lips ascends,
And grant that we may enter where
    Thanksgiving never ends.

DESOLATION.

AUTUMN is dying, coldly drear
    The wailing winds are sweeping
Adown the glen, across the fen—
    The fading flowers are weeping.

Autumn is dying, fallen leaves
    In forest paths are drifting;
The year is old, the trees, a-cold,
    Bare arms to heaven are lifting.

AUTUMN LEAVES.

Autumn is dying; forest aisles
  No more with joy are ringing;
In southern bowers, mid fadeless flowers
  The songsters, sweet, are singing.

Autumn is dying; chill and cold,
  O'er her face shadows are stealing;
In midnight drear, in solemn prayer
  By her couch, the Old Year's kneeling.

Autumn is dying; her dear face
  In the blight of death is fading;
Love's saddest strain, sorrows refrain,
  All Nature seems pervading.

Autumn is dying; loving hands
  Stretch forth in mute caressings,
And tears are shed, and her dying bed
  Is consecrate with blessings.

WANDERING.

I'D WANDERED afar from the Shepherd's fold—
The way was thorny, and dark, and cold;
My garments faded, and rent, and worn,
My feet were bleeding and brier-torn;
So long, in the forest, I'd been astray,
That I no longer could trace the way,
Sadly weeping and sore afraid,
In the perilous journey I paused dismayed.

Darkly had fallen the stormy night—
Hidden were all the stars from sight;

Wedding garments had I none,
My lamp was out, my oil was gone,
Weary, fainting and travel-soiled,
Over the barren moor I toiled;
Weeping, I came to the lonely cross
And laid in its shadow my pain and loss.

Slowly faded the darksome night,
The "Star of morn" made the pathway light,
And, humbly, I lifted my burdens once more,
And climbed the mountain and crossed the moor,
And sought again the shelter and care
Of the loving Shepherd, Who waited there
At the door of the fold; and peace and rest
I found for aye, on his loving breast.

ONLY A STEP.

ONLY A step, said a fair young child,
As she paused a moment, looked up, and smiled;
The way had seemed long to her weary feet,
As slowly she traversed the dreary street.

Only a step; the words were a sigh—
And the student raised his thoughtful eye;
The road was rough, thorns pierced his feet,
But the heights of fame his vision greet.

Only a step; my hairs are gray—
I have come a long and toilsome way;
Truth is my leader, Faith my guide,
With them I can safely cross Death's tide.

Only a step; but I have no fears—
The grave may be dark, and wet with tears—
There's a Star in the East, whose beams light the West,
And beyond is the city of endless rest.

SHALL WE KNOW EACH OTHER IN HEAVEN?

SHALL we know each other in heaven,
　　When all pain and toil are o'er?
Shall we know the friends we have loved,
　　The friends that have gone before—
　　　　To that "shining shore?"

Shall we know each other above,
　　When the grave shall give up its prey—
When the Savior shall lead his "lambs"
　　Through the silent, shadowy way,
　　　　To a land of nightless day?

Shall we know each other in heaven?
　　Ah, who would care to go,
If those we've cherished here
　　We were never more to know—
　　　　The dear friends we love so!

Shall we know each other above?
　　Ah, better an endless sleep,
Than to lose all thought of the past
　　In Eternity's great deep;
　　　　What could we do but weep?

We shall know each other in heaven—
No dear ones there to miss!
When we reach our Father's house,
There be no parting kiss,
In that world of bliss.

ASLEEP AT HIS POST.

Buried in dreams of home and friends,
Joy and hope with his vision blends,
Forgotten his toil, unheeded the blast,
To him the sleep-angel gives back the past;
Forgotten the foe encamped on the plain,
In dream-land he wanders with loved ones again;
But the roar of the cannon sounds on his ear,
And he starts up appalled with swift-rushing fear;
Alas! 'tis too late, for that terrible host
Found the sentinel-soldier asleep at his post.

And there are watchmen on Zion's tower
Unheeding the strife of the present hour,
With folded hands and careless eye,
They give no warning to passers-by;
No watchword they give as they pass along,
To the hosts led captive by pleasure's song,
Till roused from their slumbers they find with dismay,
Their foes closing round with the closing day,
And unquelled passions, a terrible host,
Take captive the watchman asleep at his post.

We are watchmen all, by the gate of Death;
Life is passing away as passes a breath.

We must fight fierce battles with selfish pride,
As we march down the sands by the river side;
Let the watchword be duty, we'll close not our eyes,
Lest the army of sin take our heart by surprise:
But the fiercer the battle the brighter the crown
We shall wear, when our earthly sun goes down,
And a glorious welcome shall greet the host
Of watchmen who ne'er fell asleep at their post.

"FATHER, GUIDE ME!"

LONELY, lonely is my pathway,
   Weary have my footsteps grown,
Reaping only pain and sorrow,
   Sad and fainting far from home!

Father! Father! hear my wailing,
   Guard and strengthen me I pray!
Teach me, guide me, lest I wander
   Blindly, weakly, from Thy way!

Guide me, guide me o'er Death's river
   When I reach its darksome tide!
Boldly, safely I may venture,
   With the Savior for my guide.

FLOWERS OF OLDEN TIME.

THE modest blue violet,
 Kissed by the soft dew,
Dwells content, since God wills it,
 In wild hedge-rows from view.
And the sweet child of nature,
 Fair allysum pale,
Half hides her shy beauty,
 In her white bridal veil.

The gay silken poppies
 Leave their dreams half untold,
· To their little French sisters,
 The bright marigold,
To watch the nasturtion,
 That flaunts overhead,
Forgetting the brown earth
 Was ever her bed.

Wake-robins and catch-fly,
 Country cousins, we think
Of the fragrant carnation,
 Sweet-william and pink.
The dahlias so stately
 In velvet and gold,
Beside the proud fox-glove
 Their glories unfold.

Red roses for youth,
 When the spirits are gay;
Purple pansies for age,
 When the hair has grown **gray;**

AUTUMN LEAVES.

Roses and smiling
  Are seemly together;
Pansies are prayerful
  In gloomiest weather.

The white lily weeps
  At the closing of day;
Does she mourn for the tempted
  Ones, going astray?
The daisy looks up
  When the still stars are shining;
And the moss, lowly creeping,
  Is ne'er heard repining.

Forget-me-nots whisper
  Of dear ones departed,
Of *one* we once loved,
  Who died, broken-hearted.
The bright morning-glory,
  That lives but an hour,
Teaches how fleeting
  Are grandeur and power.

Yet sweeter, and dearer,
  And fairer than all,
Is the pale, pink sweet-brier,
  Growing close to the wall.
In the garden of childhood,
  Where narcissus, white,
Made the shadowy nook
  A fair dream of delight.

But that home is o'ershadowed
  By Death and the Tomb,
And o'er the old garden,
  Broods the spirit of gloom.

For only in heaven,
   Are flowers blooming ever,
And only in heaven
   Friends love on forever.

THE CRY OF A LOST SOUL!

"GIVE me liberty!" the drunkard cries;
   "See you not this cursed chain?
It binds my soul to endless death;
   It burns into my brain."

The réd, red wine, see how it foams,
   Is there no rest for me?
Unloose these chains! unbind these bands!
   And set my spirit free.

O, give me liberty! it falls from lips
   All pale with coming death—
A soul's last cry, with the heart's last beat,
   And ends with the fleeting breath.

AFTER DEATH.

I'LL lay white flowers upon his breast;
The Lord has given peace and rest;
His saint-like face was fair to see,
Even after Death's Gethsemane.

Ah! did he see a vision fair,
Of angels hovering in the air?
And did he hear the anthem free,
"O, Death! where is thy victory?"

That his rapt face in slumbers deep
Should smiling lie, in dreamless sleep;
As if the opening gates of heaven,
A glory to his face had given?

For him all toil and pain is done,
He bore the cross—the victory won;
He fought—then at the battle's close
He found ineffable repose.

His glorious crown of silver hair!
His face, like marble pure and fair;
His folded hands in holy calm
Are worthy of the Martyr's palm.

I ll lay white flowers upon his breast,
Emblem of his peaceful rest;
Never more for him shall be
The pain of Death's Gethsemane.

THE PAST.

LET the dead past lie under the daisies,
   Begin life's battles anew;
Have the waters of pain baptized thee?
   In the future prove trusty and true.

Tears can not wash away sinning,
  Deeds of atonement are just;
The talent that's hid in a napkin,
  Will only be gathering rust.

Let thy life have another beginning,
  Thy service a higher aim;
Truth, and honest endeavor,
  Sanctify sorrow and pain.

Moments thoughtlessly wasted
  Are   ever mementoes of grief;
If we scatter no seed in the spring-time,
  Summer gives no blossom or leaf.

Let the dead past be ever thy lesson,
  Every day, as it goes, is a loan;
The deeds of to-day are your treasures,
  Time present is only your own.

Yesterday's dead, and to-morrow,
  For you its sun never may rise;
You have only to-day for life's roses,
  Their bloom in the even-tide dies.

The past is safe in God's keeping;
  To-day he has given in trust;
To-morrow may bring us life's ending—
  Mortality—dust shall be dust!

Who shall set bounds to the future?
  The past thy lesson must be;
Strength ever comes with the doing,
  Pruning saves many a tree.

Remember, the spirit's immortal,
   For it there's weal or there's woe;
Let thy soul-strivings ever be upward,
   For you ever must reap, as you sow.

THE UNKNOWN.

IF I could see God's will in all the sorrows
   That rise, like specters, in my darkened path;
If I could feel that all life's untold anguish
   Was sent in love, untinged with heaven's wrath,
In silence I would bow and hush complainings,
   And with an eye of faith no longer clouded,
Cling to the mighty Hand that leads me onward
   Beyond these valleys, low, and mist enshrouded.

If I, while sailing through life's stormy breakers,
   Tossed to and fro upon an ever treacherous sea,
Could hear the voice that hushed the angry surges,
   And whispered peace to wind-wracked Galilee,
I'd clasp His hand and walk upon the waters
   With feet faith-sandaled where my Lord might go—
Though walled on every side by cold and angry billows,
   Whose moan whispered of death in the dark depths below.

If I could know that when this lonely earth-life,
   With its wild phantasy of dreams, had passed forevermore,
I'd find the one dear face the green sod covers,
   Waiting to greet me, safe upon the other shore;

I'd lift the Cross with smiles—no longer weary—
 Though bending low to earth beneath the load
I'd raise my voice in notes of fullest rapture,
 Though every foot-print marked the way in blood.

AN EDITOR'S MUSING.

An EDITOR sat in his old worn chair,
A prey to every vexing care
 That makes up an editor's life.
He pondered over mysterious things,
Railroad riots and whisky rings,
Official bribes and party stings,
 Unending political strife.

His "leaders" spoke of life's strange maze—
The news, the laws, and fashion's ways;
 Politics, poetry, bread.
There were half-remembered dreams of youth,
And half-forgotten gleams of truth,
And funny jokes, and words of ruth,
 And "how shall the tramp be fed?"

Of the golden chord that ought to bind
All men as brothers, and make them kind,
 Now rusted by doubt and fear.
And he cried, "Why must the editor see
His visions of life's Utopia,
His schemes of blessing humanity
 All melt away into air?"

Then he thought of the wood's path, green and cool;
The mother's kiss as he started for school,
   To the school-house under the hill,
Where sturdy boys to manhood grew,
Taught to be honest, brave and true,
Keeping the golden rule in view—
   Joyous these memories still!

He thought of the farm house, a sacred fold,
Where loved ones gathered in days of old,
   Half covered by clambering vines;
Where ripening fields and orchards red
Fulfilled God's promise of righteous bread;
Where rose and lily their fragrance shed
   Beneath the whispering pines.

Four stalwart sons were the farmer's pride,
In youth their paths lay side by side,
   In the farm house under the pines.
How dear the memory now to him
Of the patriarch's prayer, the evening hymn,
Which his mother sang in the twilight dim,
   As sweet as vesper chimes.

John is a farmer, "wealthy and wise,"
   He, whistling, follows the plow;
No cloud on his face, no cloud in his skies,
   His happiness all must allow.

And my brother, the judge, has houses and lands,
   Of eloquent pleadings, the fee;
And Dick went to Congress, I think he forgets
   He owes some of his glory to me.

There's Elijah, the preacher, he's earning his " bread,"
  And though scorners may cavil and sneer,
He pleads for the truth, the truth of the Lord,
  With all who are willing to hear;
He counsels the living, buries the dead,
  Walks humbly in love, without fear.

And the doctor finds glory on every hand,
  Right noble, and tender, and kind
He ministers well to the poor and the old,
  Better man you never could find.

An "editor," I, and my home's poor and bare,
  My children are puny and frail;
I wonder who'll think of my hard-working wife,
  If my hand and my brain should fail?
Who'll ever remember my toilsome life,
  After my ink is pale?

Ah, surely, there's One who sees all my good,
I think that He knows I have done what I could;
And I think that the seed which I long have been sowing,
In the sunshine of heaven will forever keep growing.

THE NEXT TO DIE.

PALE death stood by the sexton's side,
Watching the grave grow long and wide,

Wide and long, and dark and deep—
Fitting bed for a dreamless sleep.

Was it a phantom flitting by,
That whispered, "who'll be next to die?"

Pale the sexton turned, and cold—
And gazed at the growing heap of mould.

Many a grave his hands had made,
And he slowly paused, with uplifted spade,

And he thought, "should I be next to die,.
Who'll make the bed where I must lie?"

Ah, what does it matter, when one is dead,
Who shall hollow the earth-cold bed?

An icy face, a form of snow,
We call it death—yet do we know

Aught of the mystery? We can not see
The spirit form. The world to be,

Like an unknown shore, in darksome night
Seems far away, to our human sight;

And the deep grave hides the holy Star,
Whose light streams out from "gates ajar."

Alas, how few, with trusting hand,
Are led by faith to the restful land!

Looking into the grave, we can find
Naught but darkness—our eyes are blind.

Looking up, we may see the light,
That lifts the veil from Death's dark night.

Out of the dust all flowers must bloom;
The path to heaven is through the tomb.

Christ is kind.   Will he let us sleep
For aye, in the silence, dark and deep?

Out of our tears our faith must grow,
Till smiling, we into the shadow go,

Led by the Hand whose power can roll
The stone from the grave of the doubting soul.

It little recks, who is next to go,
Since the Master leads, who hath loved us so;

Since the risen Savior holds each breath
In his hand divine; though we call it death,

What matter? since our Lord is love,
And death to earth, means life above.

BROTHER BEN AND I.

How OFT I turn and backward glance
  Along the dusty path of life,
And long for joys of childhood's years,
  For freedom from all care and strife:
O! would I were a child again,
To roam the fields with Brother Ben.

How oft, beneath the maple shade,
  We angled for the speckled trout,
Or sailed our rough, unpainted boat,
  With merry glee and boyish shout;
Life seemed so joyous, glad and free,
To little Brother Ben and me.

The white eggs all so deftly hid,
   Close to the eves amid the hay,
Seemed then of far more worth to me
   Than eggs of gold would seem to-day;
How oft we climbed the ladder high—
My little Brother Ben and I.

Close nestled in our garret beds,
   Our music was the pattering rain
Which fell upon the slanting roof,
   With winds to chime a loud refrain;
That garret seemed near heaven, when
I shared the room with Brother Ben.

The sparkling brook still dances on,
   The lark's sweet note rings through the glade,
The reapers sing the same old song,
   The lowing herds stand in the shade
Of the deep wood, where Ben and I
Thought the tall trees reached to the sky.

And we believed that angel bands—
   When midnight veiled the sleeping earth—
Descended from their cloud-lined halls,
   And whispered flowerets into birth;
An angel-ladder seemed each tree
To little Brother Ben and me.

Ah! childhood's cloudless, rosy hours,
   On dazzling wings flitted away,
But memory, with her magic wand,
   Recalls each sunny scene to-day;
Hand clasped in hand, I roam again,
Through flower-wreathed paths with Brother Ben.

CONTENTMENT.

THE oriole, in her hammock,
  In the sunshine softly swung,
Close by, in her hedge-row cottage,
  Brown thrush nestled her young;
    In her cunning nest,
    Her little round nest,
While a joyous song she sung.

The oriole, just as sweetly,
  Sang to her nestlings three:
"Can she be happy, I wonder,
  In her castle in yonder tree?
    In that new style nest,
    That queerly built nest,"
Said brown thrush, " I'll call and see."

"Why do you build so strangely?"
  And brown thrush paused for reply,
And gazed at the oriole's hammock
  With a mocking scornful eye,
    "A queer-built nest!
    A new-fangled nest!
From the earth 'tis far too high!"

"Why weave together these grasses,
  Through the long, long summer day?
A better nest I can teach you
  To build of the fragrant hay;
    A cunning nest!
    A little round nest!
Hid from the world away;

"'Tis a joy to sing in the sunshine,
    I'm nearer heaven's own blue
Than you in your straw-thatched cottage
    Down in the hedge-row dew.
        You've a cozy nest!
        But mine is far best!
I'm sure you must own this true."

The hammock was filled with music,
    The oriole's joy unfeigned,
And brown thrush learned a lesson,
    And this was the wisdom gained:
        "God loveth best"
        No form of nest.
Contentment and love He claimed.

And whether in cottage or castle,
    If duty be cheerfully done,
Happiness follows the doer
    And blessedness nobly won.
        So the heart finds rest!
        For God knoweth best!
If we need the shadows or sun.

NIGHT.

THROUGH the drifting darkness, falleth
    The deep hush of eventide,
Close beside me, in the shadows,
    Phantoms pale around me glide.

In the west the clouds, storm-laden,
  Hide the evening star's pure light,
And the trumpet-wind clangs fiercely,
  Herald of a stormy night.

Deepest gloom and ice-cold sorrow
  Cl ng to all that erst were dear,
And the path once bright with flowers,
  Now is dark with cypress drear.

ANSWER YOUR OWN PRAYERS.

A RICH man knelt in the morning gray,
Knelt with his wife and child to pray;
Forgetting the heathen near at hand,
He prayed for those in a foreign land:
" Let the voice of the scorner be heard no more—
Thresh thy wheat, O, Lord, on the Gospel floor.

Break every idol, bow every knee,
Let worship arise alone to thee!
Let those who go down to Ganges' tide
Be buried with Thee, the crucified;
Let thy standard wave o'er India's sand,
And thy temples be builded where idols stand.

Let the cross arise and the crescent wane,
And the Mussulmen learn Thy holy name;
On the mountain tops let the Geber's fire,
In the light of Thy truth fade and expire;
Let sinners seek the open door,
And error sink to rise no more.

Lord, bless thy servant waiting here,
Wipe from all faces the falling tear,
Clothe the naked and feed the poor,
Send Thy promise from shore to shore;
All our short comings we would confess,
Lord, hear our prayer, and hearing bless."

The rich man rose from his morning prayer,
And sipped his Mocha from China rare;
The glowing coal gave a summer heat,
The carpet was soft 'neath his slippered feet;
His wife in richest of robes was dressed—
In " basket and store " was the rich man blest.

* * * *

Across the way, feeble and old,
A widow toiled in her garret cold;
This morn her child with hunger wept;
No smoke up her fireless chimney crept:
" Surely the rich man would find it joy
To give me food for my starving boy."

Solftly she entered and stood by his chair,
But shrank as she saw his frowning stare:
" Only a crust, ' was her humble cry,
" Or my boy in his garret-home must die;
A crust, and one little stick to warm
Once more his cold and shivering form.

In your many barns are stores of grain,
Your cattle are countless on hill and plain,
Your ships at sea bear precious store,
And your coffers with gold are running o'er;
Iron and coal in your mines abound,
And wealth flows up from the yielding ground."

"Enough!" he cried, "I have naught to give!
No beggar even deserves to live!"
"Such mercy as you've shown," she said,
"God send again upon your head!"
And faint with hunger she turned away,
Too sad for tears, and too weak to pray.

"Would it make you poor to give her bread?"
The thoughtful child of the rich man said.
"Is that why you prayed for Christ to come
So far away from his starry home?
Will he bring that woman a crust to eat,
And shoes for her cold and naked feet?

I'm sure our teacher at Sunday-school
Told us to follow the golden rule;
And riches, she said, were lent, not given,
And charity, sweet, was the road to heaven—
Do you think that Jesus will come to-day
To feed those people across the way?"

*   *   *   *

O, the wisdom that falls from the lips of a child!
'Tis the Spirit's teachings all undefiled,
For their souls have so lately 'scaped from heaven,
That they bear the imprint by angels given;
Only years of contact with sordid earth
Can blot out the *Christness* God gives at birth.

*   *   *   *

For a moment the rich man hung his head
Abashed, before his child, then said:
"To-day is Christmas, peace and good will
Should fill each heart, do as you will,
My child, with my store of yellow gold
Give to the suffering, the poor, the old."

" Papa, do you mean on this Christmas day,
　To answer the prayer God heard you say? "
Then this thought crept into the rich man's brain:
" Prayer without works is worse than vain! "
Now a song goes up from the angel band—
" *See, his works with his prayers go hand in hand.*"

OUR LESSON.

THE Master dwelt in Nazareth,
　And wrought with patient hand,
The daily tasks that Joseph gave,
　Obeying each command;
Teaching the lesson, by his life,
　Which he would have us learn,
That there is work for us to do
　Whichever way we turn.

And, "floating down the stream of time,"
　His voice falls soft and clear;
Hark! you can catch the loving tone,
　If you but pause to hear,
" *Take up your cross and follow me !* "
　Ah! heavy task and drear!
But, lo! His love hath made it light,
　Behold! the skies grow clear.

No mortal, born, can ever say:
　" There is no work for me! "
For ignorance, and woe, and crime,
　On every side we see,

Calling upon the Christian heart
  For pity and for prayer,
For loving word and healing touch,
  For constant, faithful care.

The cup of water, "in His name,"
  Ah, who shall dare deny?
The warning word, the loving look,
  To mortals passing by?
We have no promise of good cheer,
  Save that which labor brings,
The sweetest songs in all the earth,
  The honest toiler sings.

To some He gives an humble sphere,
  With little earthly store,
And well He knows their many cares,
  For He was poor before.
And others are beset by woes,
  And never ending fears—
His heart can feel their every grief—
  "He was a man of tears."

All lives must have their battle field,
  Ere Mecca looms in sight;
Across all skies some clouds must rise,
  All days must have their night.
But in the darkness, 'mid the storm,
  If we but do our best,
Sweet faith will bridge the gulf that lies
  Between labor and rest.

CHRISTMAS HYMN.

" Glory to God and peace on earth,"
Proclaimed the Savior's hour of birth;
Glory to God, He reigns on high,
" Ruler alone of earth and sky."
" Peace be to man," this peace may be
Ours, through a vast eternity;
Our earthly house, by slow decay,
May fade and pass from earth away.
" Glory to God," in heavenly lands,
An everlasting mansion stands,
Where the pure river's ceaseless flood
" Makes glad the city of our God."
The stars that sang at Jesus' birth
Still circle round the rolling earth,
Still "sing together as they shine,"
Of all His majesty divine;
Shall mortal lips refuse to sing
The glory of this risen King,
Or tell the story angels told
To shepherds in the days of old—
The story of that love divine
Which naught can fathom, naught confine?
Through death's dark and shadowy land,
We shall climb where angels stand,
If we help our poorer brother,
Loving God and one another;
Following Christ, the meek and lowly—
Live as he lived, pure and holy;
Sing, as angels sang in heaven:
" Lo, the Star of Bethlehem's risen,"

Sing, as sang the stars of night;
" Lo, he comes, the Lord of Light "—
Shout aloud his glorious birth—
" Glory to God and peace on earth."

SILENT CONQUESTS.

ENCOMPASSED by sorrow, beset by sin,
Strong foes without and dark fears within,
Longing for rest, yet longing in vain,
For stretching afar is a desert plain,
And our tired feet must cross the sand,
To reach the vales of the Promised Land.

Life's broken arrows unquivered lie,
And joy expires with a long drawn sigh;
Roses must fade, and thorns alone
Are left where lately but beauty shone,
And we clasp our torn and bleeding hands,
Where beneath the cross pale Duty stands.

There are dismal swamps where the scorpion hides,
And dreary forests where death abides;
There are rivers to ford and mountains to climb,
In the noon-day heat of the summer time,
Before we can walk the everglades
Where the Lily of Sharon never fades.

By echoless graves we pause and cry,
But the moss-grown hollows give no reply;
We tread frail bridges o'er dizzy heights,

Oft led astray by unsphered lights,
Ere by the waveless stream we stand,
Dividing time from the timeless land.

We must grope through the spectral gloom of night,
When the storm-cloud hides the pale star-light,
While the tempests break on the rock-bound shore,
With sullen wail and angry roar,
Ere we gain the harbor where rainbows smile
O'er the calm, sweet waves round Eden's Isle.

TO A FRIEND ON HER THIRTY-FIFTH BIRTH-DAY.

"The days of our years are three score years and ten.

You're standing on the mountain height,
Half-way from childhood's morning light,
Half-way from death's enshrouding night,
　　　And all is well.

The hopes of early days have fled;
False lights of later years are dead;
By Wisdom's hand you now are led,
　　　And all is well.

The flowers you gathered on the way
Have withered slowly day by day;
Their beauty was too frail to stay,
　　　Yet all is well.

For fading they bequeathed to earth
An emblem of the heavenly birth,

The fragrance of undying worth,
    And all is well.

Green graves like mile-stones mark the way
To show where you have paused to say:
"Thy will be done," and knelt to pray,
    Still all is well.

Sweet Hope has led you by the hand,
Her mission ends as here you stand;
And Faith guides toward the sunset land,
    And all is well.

And faithful memory onward goes
To cheer you till the journey's close;
Forgiveness scatters all your foes,
    And all is well.

The weary toil that all must share,
Man's birthright in this world of care,
The cross which every soul must bear,
    You've borne full well.

Now standing on this mountain height,
Behold, the city greets your sight;
The vale below is filled with light,
    And all is well.

O, soul! beyond this mountain crest,
Behold thy home, thy place of rest,
O, land of Beulah! bright and blest,
    Where all is well.

MORNING PRAYER.

HEAVENLY Father, grant thy grace,
  That we may all subdue
Every sin which would efface
  Heaven and Thee from view.
Prayerfully, may we forgive,
  Those who use us ill;
And if waves of passion rise,
  Bid the waves be still.

Teach us to pardon all our foes,
  To pardon and to love;
May our hearts seek only Thee,
  And the rest above;
Toil on, hope on, with perfect faith,
  Till faith is lost in sight,
Till o'er the mountain-top we catch
  Heaven's battlements of light.

THE OLD AND NEW YEAR.

AH, New Year, do you bring to-night
Thornless roses and undimmed light?
Will your ermine mantle, your jewels rare,
With their brightness blot out pain and care?
Will the bloody sword of sin be sheathed?
Will the gates of hell be laurel-wreathed?

O, New-born Year! in your earthward flight,
Did you see the Old Year clothed in white?
On an icy bier they laid his form,
And bore him away 'mid the wintry storm.
Oh, where have they made his lonely grave!
It is hidden deep in Oblivion's cave?

Listen! the pine tree's dreary wail
Mingles and blends with the northern gale;
The wolf's a-cold in his snow-bound lair;
The owl sits glum with his eyes a-fire,
While I search in vain in midnight's gloom
'Mong shadows weird for the Old Year's tomb.

The skeleton hands ot "Long Ago"
Thrust the misspent past, with its bitter woe,
In the path my weary feet must tread,
And I hear the steps of the sheeted dead.
Others may ring their joy-bells clear,
My bells must toll for the old, dead year.

GOD IS OUR REFUGE.

" GOD is our refuge and strength, a very present help in trouble."—*Psalm xlvi.*

" God is our refuge," to Him we will fly
When the dark clouds of sorrow are gathering nigh;
When tempests of anguish about us shall roll,
He'll scatter the darkness, breathing peace to the soul.

His love is around us, He'll guard us from harm;
Wherever we wander, we shall feel His strong arm;
With garments of glory He covers the land,
And blesses His children with bountiful hand.

In God is our strength! His children he'll guide,
And keep them from evil, from folly and pride;
To the careless, the sinful who stray from His fold,
His grace is abundant, His love is untold.

" His wisdom is perfect," His promises sure;
His mercy, unfathomed, through time shall endure;
He watches His children with tenderest care,
And a home in bright mansions His hand shall prepare.

" Our strength " He will be; He taketh our hand
To lead us through death to eternity's land;
" Though the earth were removed, mountains sunk in the sea,
" He's our city of refuge," to Him we will flee.

A PRAYER FOR STRENGTH.

I DO NOT ask for rest, but strength to labor on;
I do not ask for wages, 'till the day of toil is done;
I do not ask for sunlight, but power to meet the blast,
And the Master's hand to guide me when skies are overcast.

I do not ask for wealth, for well I know, dear Lord,
I have Thy promise—"Daily bread—" as written in Thy Word;
And as I go my way alone, in sorrow's weary night,
When all earth's stars have faded, be Thou the guiding light.

I do not ask for life! but O, I long to hear
Thy loving whisper—" Peace, be still," to the dark waves of fear;
Though poverty be steeped in tears, O, make me strong to bear
The doom of woe Thou sendest me, nor doubt Thy loving care.

If I must tread the woeful paths of dread Mount Calvary,
To reach the hallowed shrine where dwells alone, Infinity;
If I must bear to watch and weep amid this life's unrest,
O, take away each broken reed and clasp me to Thy breast.

If from the harvest-fields of life I'm driven forth in pain,
If I must, weeping stand and wait, while others reap the grain,
Surely a cup of water e'en my poor trembling hand
Can offer to the toilers—the weary—working band.

E'en from the scantiest table, some little crumbs may fall,
Which will feed the tiny sparrow,—God's love is over all—
When pale lips murmur blessings tor charity that's given,
Of the motives of the giver, a record's made in heaven.

The white smoke, from the altar of self-sacrifice, will shed
A fadeless glow along the way that weary feet must tread;
The vines by martyrs planted the purple clusters bear,
And flowers, e'en in their dying, shed fragrance on the air.

From Marah's bitter waters I fain would turn away,
But if I needs must drink the cup, O, strengthen me, I pray!
" To the end I will be with you! " precious promise in our pain,
And thus the two-fold meaning of sorrow is made plain.

Earth's children, weeping ever, send forth a ceaseless moan,
Yet never, in their sorrow, do they agonize alone:
There is no obscure pathway where mortal feet may tread,
But the ever-reaching sunlight of God's smile is overhead.

SPRING.

SWEET spring has kissed the field and wood,
  The lilacs are in bloom,
The dew hides in the violet's heart,
  The rose breathes sweet perfume.
The blue-birds chatter in the trees,
  The sparrow in the hedge;
The brook is playing hide-and-seek,
  With willow-wand and sedge.

The pink has caught a fairy's heart,
  And wears it on her breast,
The daffodil and buttercup,
  Are gay in golden vest.
The blushing daisy hides her head,
  Behind her glossy leaves;
And close beside, the spider gray,
  His web of laces weaves.

Like flashing gems, the orioles
  Swing in the balsam tree;
The morning glory's stainless heart
  Enfolds the humming-bee;
The trailing myrtle's starry eyes
  Have gazed so long above,
That they have stolen from the skies
  The hue that angels love

Spring, with her thousand miracles,
  Spring, with her sweet-brier face,
Teaches lessons of holy trust,
  Teaches lessons of grace.

Patient she waits, when March winds blow;
  Patient through April showers;
Through tears she smiles and looks above,
  For heaven-promised flowers.

DOUBTING CASTLE.

Long ages ago, "Doubting-castle"
  Was built in the forest so drear;
Sorrow keeps guard at the portal;
  The warder is sable-robed Fear.

The sunlight of faith never enters;
  Love shudders, and hastens away
From the corridors mystery-haunted,
  Where the spectres of past ages stray.

The cry of the owl and the bittern
  Is heard 'mid the gloom of the night,
The storm-phantoms shriek in the gloaming,
  Where Bigotry hides from the light.

The red meteor gleams o'er the casement,
  Like grave-lights that play round the tomb;
And the tapestry hung in its chambers
  Is woven in sophistry's loom.

The death-loving spider has woven
  A shroud, o'er each fair sculptered face;
And dimmed and defaced by Time's fingers,
  The lines once by artist-hand traced.

Neither sunlight, nor beauty, nor gladness,
O'er the hearth-stone, will evermore pass;
Only woe, decked in hemlock and cypress,
Peers, skeleton-eyed, through the glass.

———

THEY SAY.

You have heard of the raven, "*Nevermore,*'
That croaked to Poe of his lost Lenore;
There's a blacker raven across the way,
Croaking forever, "They say, they say."

He hides his head from the sun's pure light,
But his voice rings out through the darksome **night—**
Let all who hear kneel down and pray
'Gainst the power of the demon-bird, "They say."

Where falsehood and envy crawl and creep,
Like poison vines in dark woods deep,
He flits, 'mid phantoms chill and gray,
Hoarsely croaking, "They say, they say."

His sharp claws tear the bleeding breast,
He drags each thought from its place of rest;
The smile on the young face fades away,
As this dark bird shrieks, "They say, they say."

Let the fair bride pause in the lightsome dance,
And the lover check his love-lit glance,
And hide, young mother, thy babe away
From the mocking fiend, "They say, they say."

Christian, thy armor may be bright,
But enter not the unequal fight—
'Twill be rent and tarnished in any fray
You may have with the loathsome bird, "They say."

There is no weapon of earthly mould,
No rest save the grave's deep bosom cold,
'Gainst the bird that battens on human prey
The demon raven, "They say, they say."

THE SEA.

"O, GLORIOUS SEA! O, glorious sea!
  'Thou art wondrous fair and great in power;'
On rocky shores thy wild waves beat,
  Round islets fair thy breakers roam.
No man may traverse the trackless path,
  That takes thee afar to thy northern home;
Afar—where an icy seal is set,
  Like a jeweled crown on thy death-cold brow,
Where winter's eternal reign begins,
  And death rides aloft on each vessel's prow.
Thou singest to me of still other lands,
  Where summer is queen of the realm of flowers,
Where thy waves are hushed to a murmur sweet,
  And love alone fills the passing hours.
I dream of those whose graves are made
  In thy wondrous caverns deep, below—
They slumber sweet in coral halls—
  Lit up by pearl's pale lambent glow."

LOVE.

"Love ye one another!"
  Con the lesson o'er
Till on the spirit's altar,
  It burns forever more.

"Love ye one another!"
  Bid every thought depart,
Which, in unguarded speaking,
  Might chill and wound the heart.

Love's the only passport.
  Across the rolling flood,
That stretches dark and cheerless
  Between us and our God.

"Love ye one another!"
  'Twas whispered long ago,
By One who came to show us
  The way that we must go.

Divinely born and uttered,
  These words from God on high,
Form the star-lit ladder,
  We climb to reach the sky.

They're the "Law and Prophet;"
  They make the "Gospel plan;"
They shadow forth the glory
  That heaven holds for man.

THE DYING YEAR.

Toll, toll, midnight bells, toll for the year that's dying;
Underneath a snowy shroud his aged form is lying;
　　North-winds wailing, hemlock trailing,
Over the couch of the year that's dying,
Over the form in grave-clothes lying.

Toll, toll, midnight bells, King Death his court is keeping;
Another year, another year in Time's cold vault is sleeping;
　　North-winds wailing, moonbeams paling
Over the grave of the cold dead year:
Over the form on its snowy bier.

VIOLETS.

The precious violets wet with dew
Of modest worth are emblems true;
They've caught the color of the skies,
And hold it in their sweet blue eyes;
O, learn of them that virtue dwells
In lowly homes and forest dells.

THE ROSE.

'Tis said, the rose was ever white,
Until in Gethsemane, at night,
The Savior bathed the flowers in blood
From drops that on his forehead stood.

THE DOVE AND THE CHERUB.

A CHERUB on a summer's day,
From heaven had wandered far away—
A tiny cherub bright and fair,
With azure wings and golden hair.

He sported 'mid heaven's cloud-lined halls,
And danced upon the waterfalls,
Where rainbow spray gave back the light
Like flashing diamonds pure and bright;

Then, growing weary, sought the dell,
And creeping in a lily-bell,
In peaceful slumber closed his eyes,
And wild bees hummed his lullabies.

But storm-clouds dimmed the sun's fair light,
The cherub woke in sore affright,
And cried aloud in wild dismay:
" The sunny hours in idle play
Were passed; now comes the hour of gloom—
My work unfinished, far from home
I wander, lost, nor know the way,
And evening brings the closing day."

Just then the storm-cloud opened wide,
A snow-white dove flew to his side
Harnessed with bands of heavenly light,
And pinions quivering for flight.

He hailed the dove with rapture wild,
And through his tears looked up and smiled;
Then hasted toward the setting sun,
To do the work he'd left undone.

The cherub's mission led him where
A wail rose on the evening air,
From one who wept above a bier—
He checked his flight and whispered clear:

" Your darling rests—though dark the gloom,
Arise, and gaze above the tomb! "
The mourner saw the white-winged dove,
And heard the cherub's voice of love;
Her heart grew calm, she hushed her fears,
And radiant smiles shone through her tears.

They heard, above the city's din,
The sweet notes of an evening hymn;
A saint's glad anthem, loud and clear,
The cherub paused and lingered near.

He saw, in Azriel's presence chill,
The Christian's form grow pale and still,
But caught his smile of faith and love—
His whispered, " There is rest above."

Once more he paused; this time to win
A soul from paths of shame and sin;
Then passing through the star-lit night,
Reached heaven's gates of pearly white.

Low knelt the cherub at the throne:
" Father, this truth I fain would own,
True happiness is only found,
In all the universe around,
By those who seek to do thy will,
And all thy great commands fulfill;
And only such can hope for rest
In the bright mansions of the blest."

The dove this message took to earth;
The cherub, child of heavenly birth,
Enrobed in light and seen afar,
Mortals have named, "The Evening Star."

MAY AND I.

MAY is dressed in costly raiment,
    In fabrics rich and rare,
And diamonds are on her lily hands,
    And pearls in her raven hair.

Stately and cold she passes,
    Drawing her robes aside,
Lest she touch with the hem of her garment,
    One she scorns in haughty pride.

My hands are brown with toiling;
    My garments plain and old;
Yet, of far more worth are *my* treasures,
    Than all of her stores of gold.

Gone, her father and mother;
    Gone, brothers and sisters — all —
She, alone, in her icy grandeur,
    Reigns in the gloomy hall.

I have a darling mother
    Asleep in her easy chair,
Where the shimmering fire-light brightens
    The waves of her whitening hair.

I have a dear old father
  Who shields me with tender love;
On earth *one* brother, *one* sister,
  And loved ones waiting above.

She in her lordly castle
  Is dwelling unloved, in state;
Thank God, for the lowly cottage
  That saveth me such a fate!

Would *I* have her gold and diamonds!
  Her parks and the ancient hall,
In exchange for the friends I cherish,
  And the love that is over all?

Ah! *mine* are the truest riches;
  For Love, the Alchemist rare,
Turneth all ills into blessings,
  And shieldeth the heart from care.

THE SECRET.

THE robin just told her lover,
  The wind caught up the refrain,
And told the bee in the clover,
  Who whispered it once and again
To wildwood and garden flower,
  To the heart's-ease upon the lea,
To the ivy upon the tower
  Of the castle beside the sea.

Like an emerald on waves white-crested
  An ivy leaf floated away,
And neither paused nor rested,
  Till night on the waters lay.
But a lily, in fragrant dreamings,
  Asleep in the sea's embrace,
Awoke and read the secret
  In the glance of his beaming face.

Her perfumed prayers uplifting,
  She kissed the sea of blue,
In her pure glory drifting,
  To death she passed from view.

But the mermaid caught the glory
  That glowed in her raptured eye,
From her fainting lips the story
  Which made her joy to die.

    *   *   *   *

Safe hid in a ruby sea cave, a star-fish heard the tale;
He flashed through the circling waters, nor paused for the wild-
    est gale;
And wherever he sailed, like lightning the story flamed and
    glowed,
And Neptune listened and told it, in the gloom of his dark
    abode.

Then Gnomes sped away to the ice-land, where with spears and
    glit'ring shields,
They traversed the crystal desert and swept o'er the snow white
    fields,
Till they reached where the clouds of midnight,
        Touched the pole with Erebus-hands,
Where known and unknown uniting
        In the region of mystery stands.

The clouds, as they listened, grew darker, till a flash like a river
    of light,
Proclaimed Aurora borealis the Queen of the northern night;
Then her "army with banners" went marching down the fields
    of unlimited space,
And so, in that ærial journey the secret was carried—
Was carried to stars and planets,
      And whispered through earth and air;
It flashed in the summer lightning,
      And blushed in the rosebud fair.

      The secret! man never may know it,
        'Tis a wonderful, wordless song,
      Which Nature teaches her children;
      . To her realm does the secret belong.
      Perhaps 'tis a voice of thanksgiving
        To Him who creates by His word,
      A voice from Eternity's fountain,
        By sin-deafened mortals unheard;
      We know only this, wordless anthems,
        Through Nature, must reach Nature's God.

IDOL WORSHIP.

WE pray for those who bend the knee
    To idols, in a far off land,
Lament their darkened distiny
    Who dwell where Ganges laves the strand,
And fain would scatter Christian light
In climes o'erspread by heathen night,
Plant semaphores where darkness reigns—
Where superstition winds her chains.

We pity those whose children fall
  A prey to wild beasts in their lair,
And shudder that the mother-love
  Gives sacrifice as well as prayer;
And dreams her god accepts the child
She places in the jungle wild,
Or sends afloat in bamboo bark,
Cradled upon the water dark.

We know, in truth, the funeral pyre
  Consumes the living with the dead;
In pitying tears we turn aside,
  And leave the pages half unread,
Which breathe the dark and murderous tale
Of widows burned in Siam's vale,
Or buried with the mouldering dead,
The grave their last sought bridal bed.

We, too, are idol worshipers,
  While gazing 'cross the Indian Sea,
And there are heathen dark and blind
  In cultured, proud America.
Yes, there are Arabs in the streets,
And Magdalenes with faltering feet,
That wander on in sin and night—
What hand shall lead them up to light?

We bow to Baal! We are not free!
  Alas, we share the Hindoo's crime,
And join with idol worshipers
  In this Bible-lighted clime.
Behold the red light o'er the way,
Where men their souls in madness slay,
Where grape-crowned Bacchus throned above
Demands their hopes, their lives, their love.

Why wonder, then, when low in dust
  The Brahman to *his* idol bows,
Or reverences a million gods,
  And pays to Vishnu holy vows,
When here men make a god of wine,
And mar the image once divine?
The Brahman only does the same
To idols with another name.

What means the gambler's phrenzied eye,
  When on the altar reared to chance
He stakes his every hope of heaven,
  Nor gives to God one backward glance?
No Brahman yields *his* idol more
Than love, and life, and golden store;
No fabled god by Ganges waves
Lures victims on to darker graves.

Have we no idols?   Watch the throng
  Who gather at the open door,
Where Can-can revels on the boards,
  And music from the viols pour.
The devotee here brings his gold
In summer's heat in winter's cold—
Whatever life holds pure and fair,
He smiling gives the idol there.

No idols! when the greed for gold
  Makes man forget his brother's weal,
And grasp the purse with Judas hand,
  Willing to bribe, or cheat, or steal!
The promised Truth, to make men free
Must in *all* men a brother see—
Must, entering into heart and brain,
Drive out self-love and love of gain,

And feel that men are brothers all,
  " Fallen, perhaps, but brothers still,"
Needing some hand to lift them up,
  And stay their feet from paths of ill.
Are we from idol worship free?
Come, gaze upon this human sea,
That moves in restless waves along
The streets, where fashion rules the throng!

" Look at the churches? " Ah, I see
  Where sunlit spires reach to the clouds,
Where silk-robed worshipers enthrong,
  Where eloquence holds sway o'er crowds;
But 'tis not gospel truth I hear,
From lips that drink of fountains clear,
But foamy words of modern school,
Dipped from Tradition's muddy pool.

The churches!   Luxury and pride
  Opens the door and enters there,
While poverty, bowed down in tears,
  May find no place to kneel in prayer,
In these vast piles of granite gray,
Gorgeous with gold, with purple gay;
From arch to aisle, above, around,
No room for humble worth is found.

And do not we who know the Truth,
  Drift idly on in careless ease,
Giving a mite of time or gold,
  Striving our conscience to appease?
Those who believe, their faith should **prove;**
'Tis not enough to deal out love
In homœopathic doses small,
For *Jesus* died alike for all.

A wondrous charge the Master gave:
  "Disciples! brethren! feed my sheep!"
And thrice again, "Feed thou my lambs!"
  Then, rouse ye! rouse ye! from your sleep,
For, lo! the lambs have wandered far,
With neither shelter, food, nor care;
The fold, unguarded, falls a prey
To wolves that watch for those that stray.

Let those who listen, ask their hearts
  How much of Christ-life they possess?
Lest some are drunken by your wine,
  Do you refuse the grape to press?
Will you your brother's weakness hold
Above the tempter's offered gold,
Lest you should cause your brother sin?
For drunkards may not enter in.

And, Christian women, do you pause
  Before you speak the word of blame,
Lest the last spark of hope you crush,
  And wreck a soul in sin and shame?
Remember! only those may cast
A stone who, in their whole life past,
Have kept their robes spotless and white—
E'en they should pray: "*Lord, give me light!*"

For, happen, if blind pride should guide
  The hand which holds the stone of wrath,
The zeal which would thus conquer ill
  Might worse obstruct another's path,
And cause a soul to turn away
Who else had found the better way;
And woe to those who thus offend
The weary feet that might ascend.

Whichever way we turn our eyes,
   Work for the Master we shall find;
Diamonds uncut, marble unhewn,
   A healing touch for eyes now blind;
From garden beds to pluck the rue,
And plant the morning-glory blue;
Who toils for man, in faith sublime,
Holds consecrate God's holy shrine.

A soul, the all in all of man,
   The clinging dross of earth may hide,
But who shall tell the worth of that
   For which the Infinite hath died?
The farmer does not plant his field
Expecting thorns the grape to yield,
Nor turn the furrow and then sow
The thistle, thinking flowers will grow.

Yet to this lesson, old and plain,
   Mankind will pay but little heed,
Or in the mind of every child,
   They'd pause to sow the gospel seed,
Nor leave the soil to careless hands,
Or idle winds, or drifting sands,
Or wasting passion's typhoon blight,
Or superstition's gloomy night.

Dear mothers, count your jewels o'er,
   And keep them safe from falsehood's ill,
And learn of Him who loveth much,
   And wait upon His perfect will;
And know that He who gave will ask,
Their safe return when time is past;
And, mother, think your labor light
If you but save the diamond bright,

O, Christian preacher, ponder well,
  Whether the lesson you would teach
Is one to make life's duties plain,
  One that from heart to heart will reach,
Lest traveling in the car of thought,
The letters on the fancy wrought,
With touch too light for hearts to feel,
Some messenger of Doubt may steal.

Oh, if my weak and feeble voice
  Could sound the trumpet of alarm!
My hand tear off the blinding mask
  Which Vice assumes to work her charm!
If those who walk in flowery ways
Could on the hidden serpent gaze,
They'd turn aside in wild dismay,
To Duty's mountain steep and gray.

But while we love our native shores,
  And work for souls with purpose true,
Shall we forget the Island band
  Who stretch their longing hands in view?
Shall missionaries plead in vain
For pittance of our golden grain?
Oh, let us lift our banner white,
That leads them up to gospel light!

We know that 'mid life's changing scenes,
  Who plants the smallest seed in tears
Shall see it bloom and bear its fruit,
  Enriching all the coming years.
God's promises before us rise,
A ladder reaching to the skies,
And he who sows in faith sublime,
Shall gather at the harvest time.

And if alone the gleaner's prize
   Is left where many hands have wrought;
If lonely-hearted you have bound
   The sheaves that others left unsought,
Whether you gleaned on mount or plain,
The Lord accepts your golden grain; •
And when the harvest day is done,
He'll welcome thee to " harvest home."

Then faithful sow and faithful reap,
   The truth He gives to thee;
Watered by blood from Calvary,
   This Truth shall make thee free.

———

JESUS OF NAZARETH.

WHEN Jesus, in the wilderness,
   In sore temptation prayed,
The angels ministered to him
   And Satan fled dismayed.
He taught the waiting multitude,
   " As he sat beside the sea,"
Among the humble fishermen,
   On the shores of Galilee.
     But of all his loving labors,
       There's none the heart so thrills,
     As when he blessed the children,
       Among Judean hills.

To all the people he proclaimed:
   " The kingdom is at hand;"

Tempestuous waves and winds obeyed
  The voice of his command.
God's "Great Evangel" to the poor,
  Yet poorer still than they,
He broke for them the bread of life,
  He knelt with them to pray.
    Yet of all his loving labors,
      None are so dear, so sweet,
     As when he blessed the children,
      That gathered at his feet.

To blinded eyes he gave the light
  Till they could on him gaze,
And see the tender pitying love
  Which glorified his face;
Forgave the sins of her who knelt
  And washed his feet with tears;
Met icy death and broke his bonds,
  Conquering the grave's dark fears.
    Yet the sweetest, dearest story,
      Where all have priceless charms,
     Is when he blessed the children,
      As he took them in his arms.

While Martha wept, and Mary prayed,
  He spake—their pulses thrill—
"Come forth!" and lo, their brother, dead,
  Obeyed the Master's will.
The leper, palsied, lame and dumb,
  Touched by his healing hand,
Acknowledged him their Lord and King,
  Throughout the "Holy Land."
    But of all his loving labors,
      There's none the heart so thrills,
     As when he blessed the children,
      Among Judean hills.

FAREWELL.

Farewell, Old Year, farewell!
  My tears fall thick and fast,
For sadly tolls the funeral knell,
  O'er joys forever past.

My graves are dark and deep,
  And with a breaking heart,
My vigils I must sadly keep,
  From all the world apart.

The sacred flower of love
  Has withered at thy breath,
And Hope, the wandering dove,
  Folded her wings in death.

Friendship, a-chill, lies low,
  With blood-drops on her breast;
"Faithless"—for such I know,
  Earth holds no place of rest.

Faith sadly weeps with me,
  O'er broken hopes and dreams,
Whelmed 'neath despair's dark sea,
  Where grave-light only gleams.

Farewell! the parting hour
  Has come for you and me;
I take life's burdens up once more,
  Though dark the way may be.

My Father sends the cross!
  "He doeth all things well!'
As gain I'll count all pain and loss;
  Farewell, Old Year, farewell.

THE DEATH MARCH.

"KING ALCOHOL" marches with giant tread
   His band an unnumbered host,
Over mountain, through peaceful vale,
Wherever he pauses goes up a wail
   For husbands or brothers lost.

The floods of the sea can ne'er efface
   The blood from the path they tread;
A skeleton pyramid rises high
Where the countless army passes by,
   Marching on to the realms of the dead.

All vain is the mother's love-kiss warm
   To rescue her wayward child,
He breaks from the hold of her clasping hand,
 . From the clinging love of the household band,
Drowning reason in frenzy wild.

The power of the strong man ebbs away,
   His pulses beat faint and low,
He heavily draws his trembling breath
As he follows the standard-bearer, Death,
   And his bounding step grows slow.

The fire is quenched on the cottage hearth
   By the tyrant's poisonous breath;
The plow of the farmer idly rusts,
The student's books are dim with dust—
   They've joined the march of death.

Must the holiest "light" the Lord hath made,
   Like the flashing meteor die?

Must fettered souls in gloom expire,
To build the ghastly funeral pyre,
  Which is blazing to the sky?

Alas! for mourners who watch and pray
  O'er the slain on this field of blood,
Or over the prisoners bound in chains,
Or held in dungeons where madness reigns,
  Forgetful of home or God.

Alas for the Nation! Let heaven's bell toll
  Over youth and virtue lost;
Let it rouse the dreamers, till men of might,
With Hellenic thunders, shall put to flight
  The vanguard of Satan's host.

JUNE.

Sweetest daughter of the year,
Sunny, flower-wreathed June is near;
In her foot-prints, wet with dew,
Violets spring, with eyes of blue.
Tangled song of wren and thrush
Greet us from the lilac bush,
While in fragrance, at our feet,
Fall the apple blossoms sweet.
Like scattered pearls the clover bloom
Encrowns the brow of smiling June;
Roses in her hand she brings—
In the hedge the robin sings.

The dandelion's curls of gold
Are mingled in a mazy fold,

With the strawberry's crimson sheen,
And waving grasses cool and green.
O'er tiny lake, neath cypress tall,
Sunlight and shadows shifting fall;
Embosomed on the water deep,
The white-souled lily falls asleep.
From mossy glade and bosky dell
Steals music, like a fairy bell
In joyous notes, the feathered throng
Thanking God for gift of song.

THE FISHERMAN SONG.

I HAVE wandered since the dawning
  On the ocean's wave-washed shore—
In my heart a deathless longing
  Must dwell forever more;
For where the wild waves glisten,
  They kiss my darling fair,
My lost love, Madeline, with wavy, golden hair.
    She is sleeping, ever sleeping,
      Dreamless and fair,
    My lost bride, Madeline,
      With wavy, golden hair.

I watch the tempests gather
  Across the darkening sky,
The wild winds, like a feather,
  Toss white waves mountain high;
But the lightning's quivering flashes
  Can not wake my darling fair,

My lost love, Madeline, with wavy, golden hair.
　　She is sleeping, ever sleeping,
　　　　'Mid pearls so rare,
　　　My long lost Madeline,
　　　　With wavy, golden hair.

　　　Heart-broken, sad and weary,
　　　　I linger on the shore,
　　And list the waves so dreary
　　　Murmur, "forever more
We hold within our keeping
　　　Your jewel, pure and rare,
Your lost bride, Madeline, with wavy, golden hair.
　　　In her ocean-bed she's sleeping
　　　　Free from earth's care,
　　　Your lost bride, Madeline,
　　　　With wavy, golden hair."

THE OCEAN.

They that go down to the sea in ships, that do business in great waters, these
see the works of the Lord, and his wonders in the deep.　*Psalm cvii: 23, 24.*

THE white winged ship obeys the helm,
　　And cleaves the sea in twain,
While the sailor reads the starry scroll
　　That makes his pathway plain;
As the prophet read the tyrant's fall
　　In letters of burning light,
The lonely mariner on the deep
　　Thus guides his bark aright.

Where coral-workers rear their towers,
   And build their ophal caves,
The wrecks of centuries mouldering lie,
   Deep in the unfathomed waves.
While foam-crowned breakers requiems sing
   For those in ocean-bed,
Asleep, 'till the Master's voice shall call
   To the sea: "Give up thy dead."

The northern lights, the whirlpool's roar,
   The tempest in its might,
The sea-fires shining 'cross the waves
   When storm kings rule the night—
The icebergs floating mountain high,
   The snow clouds darkling frown,
Bespeak God's power, to puny men
   Who to the deep go down.

To those who walk Time's phantom shores,
   Filled with life's sad unrest,
Watching for ships that never come
   From "Islands of the Blest,"
Faith points to sun-crowned mountain heights
   Across the valley chill,
While to our fears, as to the waves,
   Christ whispers: "Peace, be still!"

OVERSHADOWED.

Is THY way with thorns thick sown?
Are thy flowers with weeds o'ergrown?
Do the clouds which o'er thee rise,
Hide the blue of summer skies?
Have friends you trusted turned aside,
Filled with scorn, distrust or pride?

Have the years left bitter trace
Of pain and sorrow on thy face?
Has thy hair's once sunny glow
Turned to flecks of winter snow?
Have the eyes which once were bright
Lost in tears their happy light?

Where music once the hearth-stone blessed,
Do the harp-strings silent rest?
Do the buds of promise lie
Withered beneath a storm-wracked sky?
From the chill of wintry day
Have the song-birds fled away?

Do the waves of anguish roll,
"Tempest-tossed" across thy soul?
Has time stretched his fateful hand
And scattered wide thy household band?
Does the grave's dark chambers hide
All that made life's joy and pride?

Is there not one ray of light
To pierce the darkness of thy night?
Is there not a silver bow,
Rich with Truth's effulgent glow?

Is there no tracery of gold,
Lining the black cloud's deepest fold?

Will He who heeds the sparrow's fall,
Refuse His children when they call?
Lift up your eyes and catch the gleam,
Of Bethlehem's Star across the stream.
God's love creates a ladder bright,
Which spans the gloom of death and night.

And though below, the surges roll,
The Savior's voice the waves control;
Lay at His feet your stubborn will
And hear Him whisper: "Peace, be still!"
While love and mercy bending down,
Place on your brow a star gemmed crown.

THE LAND OF BEAUTY.

THERE'S beauty in the sunshine
    That gilds with radiant light,
The clover-blooming meadows,
    And mountain's lofty height;
That braids with gold, the willow,
    And kisses into birth
The flowers of vale and hillside,
    To wreathe the waiting earth.

There's beauty in the moonbeam,
    That floats on silver wing,
To wake the dreaming lilies
    With promises of spring—

In rivers hastening, ever,
  To meet the waiting sea,
Catching the rainbow's colors,
  From sky, and flower and tree.

With joy the thrush and blue-bird
  Sound through the forest aisle
Their sweet songs of thanksgiving,
  While bud and blossom smile;
And all the groves are stirring
  To wind-harp anthems free,
And Aspen tassels quiver
  With the wild minstrelsy.

The hand of God, with beauty,
  Has traced His great design
Upon the blushing rose-leaf
  And mountain cliff sublime;
But earth, with all its brightness,
  Grows pale, and dim, and cold,
Compared with heavenly glory
  Shut in by gates of gold.

THE SWALLOWS' WELCOME.

BRIGHT little swallows, welcome once more,
Your long winter wanderings safely are o'er:
Flitting so fearlessly, on purple wing,
Sweet to our hearts is the promise you bring.

'Neath the low eaves your cottage you'll find,
Safe where you placed it, untouched by the wind;
Its portals of clay, half hidden from view,
By the widespreading arms of the mossy old yew.

Now you're darting aloft to the blue of the skies,
Beyond the fond gazing of all mortal eyes,
Then gracefully floating from cloud-land afar,
With your wings all a-quiver and eyes like a star!

If like *thee*, forgetting our houses of clay,
We could rise 'bove the clouds, obscuring our way,
And gather from heaven stores of patience and grace,
We'd nevermore falter at life's darkest place.

What though we dwell in the lowliest cot,
Scorned by proud worldlings, by others forgot;
If no songs of rapture our voices can raise,
Even silence is sometimes the soul of all praise.

Ah, bird of the pilgrims, with faith like to thine,
We can make of our earth-life a picture sublime;
For the end of all wisdom is sweetest content,
Whether sunshine or clouds on our pathway are sent.

DECEMBER.

DECEMBER—bitter and cold and drear,
Is weaving a shroud for the dying year;
Weaving a shroud of the snow-flakes white,
Weaving alone through the silent night.

Souls in smiling, and souls in tears,
Have watched the flight of the passing years;
And many sin-stained, a-tremble with fright,
Would stop Time's shuttle's unceasing flight.

While others rejoice that the weaver gray,
In each thread of the warp has numbered a day—
Each thread of the woof a good deed done—
Life's web shows fair in the setting sun.

While the weaver is counting each passing hour,
The bells in the snow-wreathed, ice-covered tower
Are chiming the story of Him whose birth
Brought light and life to the death-dark earth.

"My heart is a-chill," the weaver cries,
While the half-filled shuttle he swiftly plies;
"My hour approaches, this broken thread
Must be mended by other hands instead."

His voice falls faint on the midnight air;
And the pearl-gemmed shroud so pure and fair
Covers the child and his white-haired sire,
For December lies dead with the old dead year.

RESTORED.

THE rain is drearily falling,
  And the pine trees' restless moan
Makes me shiver and tremble,
  As I sit by the hearth alone.

Out from the growing shadows,
  March spectres to and fro,
And memory's hall is crowded
  With scenes of long ago.

First the form of my lover—
  My lover now, as then—
Who sailed away in the sunlight,
  My beautiful Marmiden.

The brave old ship was shattered
  And lost in a northern gale;
'Twas just such a storm as this is,
  Just so did the pine trees wail.

As I list to the call of the breakers,
  I long for the restful sleep,
Where heart-pain is hushed forever,
  In eternity's infinite deep.

I dream, and my dreams are of heaven,
  For I meet with the loved ones again,
Bodies, not spirits, are fettered
  To earth, by mortality's chain.

The firelight fades, and darkness
  Gathers around me, sombre and chill,
And I long for power, like the Master,
  To whisper: "Peace, be still;"

To whisper *peace* to the ocean,
  Hoarse beating the rock-ribbed shore—
To whisper *peace* to the longing
  Of my sad soul, evermore.

Hark! they are ringing the church bells,
    They tolled them a year to-night,
For the loss of the crew and captain,
    Of the good ship, Northern Light.

A step! 'tis the step of my lover—
    Not dead! thank God! the sea,
From out the gloom of the tempest,
    Has given him back to me.

The rain is still drearily falling,
    In the pine trees the winds still wail,
But my sailor is sitting beside me,
    And I heed not the fiercest gale.

THE BLUE BIRD.

A LITTLE bird with a bright blue coat,
This spring came chanting his musical note:
Like silver bells the changes rang,
And soft and clear was the song he sang;
Beautiful bird with azure wing,
First and fairest prophet of spring.

He sang of the golden hours of May,
Of ferny dells where shadows play,
Of fragrant lilies bathed in dew,
Of budding roses and violets blue;
He sang, unheeding April showers;
He sang to waken the dreaming flowers.

He sang at the pearly gates of day,
While shadows crept o'er the hills away;
The echoing music softly fell
Like childhood's dream of a fairy bell;
A chorus so wild, so deep, so strong,
That space o'erflowed with the wine of song.

Naught to him was the leafless tree,
Cheery, and brave and bright was he,
And the purple clouds on the mountain crest,
Where golden arrows of sunrise rest,
Seemed a cathedral grand and tall,
With the granite hills for tower and wall.

And the birdling's wild and wayward song
Grew to an anthem deep and strong,
That told ot Love, and Hope and Heaven,
And the peace that comes to the sin-forgiven
Who catch the gleam of light that lies
Beyond the gates of Paradise.

Ah! woodland preacher, such hopes you wake,
My soul its bondage longs to break;
I marvel not that men of old
Believed all music God controlled,
Since weary years fade like a dream,
And faith and hope are life supreme.

"As is thy day, thy strength shall be,"
Through thy sweet song God speaks to me;
In wintry hours or shades of night,
With heart bowed low by sorrow's blight—
What brooks the pain of life's short way,
Since death is life's unending day!

LITTLE SUNBEAM.

LITTLL SUNBEAM, darling sunbeam,
　Flitting through this world of care,
Lighting up its dreary places,
　Till it seems an Eden fair.

Little sunbeam, darling sunbeam,
　Prattling gaily through the day,
Gathering roses from the bowers,
　Shaking dew-drops from the spray.

Little sunbeam, darling sunbeam,
　Sweeter than the roses are—
Song of robin, song of blue-bird,
　With thy notes hath no compare!

Little sunbeam, gentle sunbeam,
　Christ hath blessed thee, joyous child:
Oh, may angels guard and keep thee
　Ever sin-free, undefiled!

ONLY TEARS TO GIVE.

You ASK for a song—I can give but tears,
Tears for the loved ones gone before—
While lonely and sad, on the wind-swept **shore**,
I wander and gaze at the surging tide,
And long to pass to the other side.

Ah, a wailing song—and the tune must be
Sad as the moan of the restless sea
When the cloud-king rides on the breakers' foam,
And storm-beat ships o'er the waters roam.

You ask for a song—I can give but tears,
For all I hear is the sexton's bell,
Ringing, forever, a funeral knell;
And the preacher's voice: "Let mourners pray!"
"The Lord who gave hath taken away."
The oak can ne'er return to the vine,
But the broken tendrils must upward climb
Till they reach the throne—no death is there,
And love—dear love, rich fruit shall bear.

You ask for a song—I can give but tears,
My heart is faint in the house of prayer,
For the sight of a crown of silver hair,
For the sound of a voice, forever still,
Which could touch the heart—the pulses thrill;
Where the light from the gothic windows falls,
I can see only coffined form and pall,
And the song in silence dies away,
And shadows darken the light of day.

You ask for a song—I can give but tears.
For me no buds can ever bloom,
Save the asphodel around the tomb.
Earth is naught: "Heaven is home."
To sorrow no more; no more to roam.
What thought so sweet, so fraught with joy:
"Sin can not enter"—no pain destroy!
O! days fly swift on the wings of prayer,
For my soul would haste to enter there!

LOST AND SAVED.

Lost, a fragment of beauty, a half-broken rhyme,
A dream, a fair flower, a moment of time,
Opportunities golden, a glimmer of fame,
A phantom of hope, an unuttered name.

Lost, the boat that was launched on a treacherous stream,
The joyous fulfillment of love's hallowed dream;
The light of a home, the love of a life;
The hope which upheld when sorrow was rife.

Lost, an "undying" promise, the bitter-sweet leaf
Of the record of hopes. The half-ripened sheaf,
Gathered too quickly, 'mid darkness and fears,
Hid away from the sunlight and baptized with tears.

Saved, the hope of a glory, unshadowed by fear,
The light of a morning undimmed by a tear;
The faith that looks upward to God as a friend,
The heaven where peacefulness never shall end.

Saved, the dream of a city where loving ones wait
'Till angels shall open the "beautiful gate"—
While we cross o'er the river so stormy and wide—
Oh! the lilies that bloom on the heaven-bright side!

Saved, the faith in the Master who stood by the sea,
Calling to weary ones: "Come unto me!"
Calling the way-worn: "Come and be blest;
Lay aside all that cumbers and enter thy rest."

MY DREAM.

I DREAMED I roamed the halls that lie
Beyond night's azure conopy;
I neared the star-lit dome sublime,
Where cycling suns in glory shine.
The milky-way, for angel feet,
I found was but the golden street,
And humbly there I paused to wait
Where the pale seraph barred the gate.

Beside the gate a gray haired man
Waited " for blessing or for ban."
" Master," he said, " I taught the way
To gain the realms of endless day.
No mystic rules, no man-made creed,
I knew could reach the sinner's need.
With zeal I preached the gospel plan
Revealed by Christ to fallen man.

I loved not power or wealth or fame,
My all was hid in Jesus' name;
I only sought for Bible light
To guide me through the grave's dark night.
' Christian ' I wrote in gleaming gold
Upon our banner's sacred fold.
Up the same path, see fearless throngs,
Bear the same name, sing the same songs!

While gazing on this scene, I stood,
A voice (was it the voice of God?)
Proclaimed : " A Christian outside waits,
Lift up your heads, ye pearly gates;

Angels through Heaven the tidings bear,
A new-born star night's brow shall wear:
Bring robes for him, bright as the sun,
And bring the crown his faith hath won.

He bore on earth a heavy cross,
And for my name he suffered loss;
He clothed the naked, fed the poor,
For sinners op'ed the gospel door;
He conquered pride, envy and sin,
That he the gate might enter in.
Behold, the Christian seeketh rest,
And finds it on the Savior's breast."

No longer weary, faint, and lone,
Our brother stood before the throne,
But in the gardens of delight,
With loved ones dressed in pearly white,
Sang the new song, to mortals given,
Who through great sorrow enter heaven;
Bewildering bliss, beyond control,
Touched with celestial fire his soul.

God loved the world—He gave his son
Jesus, "so loved," the deed was done;
And man's redeemed by love divine—
In heaven love's chain all hearts entwine;
And, loving God, man gains the prize,
Eternal life beyond the skies;
For Love is God, and God is Love,
And Love rules in the courts above.

CHARITY.

AT YOUR door sweet Charity's knocking;
  Let her in, and the angels will come
And cheer you with heavenly music
  On your march to your heavenly home.

To give to the needy is blessed,
  To labor for Christ is sublime,
The good that you do unto others,
  Will live in all coming time.

IN MEMORY

Of Sister Mary B. Howells of Cincinnati, Ohio, one of the most loving, faithful friends God ever gave me. Her life was the perfectness of religious thought, and the exemplification of all the virtues of Christianity.

IT IS not long—not long ago—
Since I clasped her hand at even-tide;
  Since, with bated breath and kindling eye,
  She talked of the golden streets, that lie
Beyond the clouds, on the other side
  Of the death-cold stream, whose dreary moan,
  En-chilled our hearts, as she passed alone
  Across the waves. "Nay, friends, why weep?
' He giveth his beloved sleep! ' "

It is not long—not long ago—
Since the voice we loved was hushed for aye,
  Since the thoughtful brow by death was paled,
  The violet eyes so softly veiled,
And the lips we kissed were turned to clay!
  A vision of memory, sweetly fair,
  Oft kneels with n.e at the evening prayer,
    Whispering, while I sad vigils keep:
  "He giveth his beloved sleep!"

It is not long—not long ago—
Since she calmly sank to dreamless rest,
  Now, twining ivy and eglentine;
  The pale sweet-brier and cyprus vine,
Have woven a wreath upon her breast.
  Oft, in the watchings of sorrow's night,
  I catch a gleam of her robes of light,
    Or list her voice at midnight deep:
  "He giveth his beloved sleep!"

It is not long—not long ago—
Yet the elder bloom, milk white and sweet,
  Kisses the marble; and roses fair
  And woodbine, with purple jewels rare,
Twine with the grasses around her feet.
  While for us, sad years must come and go,
  'Tis hers the joys of heaven to know.
    We hear across the silence deep:
  "He giveth his beloved sleep!"

It is not long—not long to wait—
'Till lengthening shadows westward fall,
  'Till across the restless waves of time,
  Will fall the sound of the death-bell's chime,

'Til we'll hear the waiting boatman call,
 And find, past the river's sullen flow,
 Friends who passed o'er not long ago—
  There saddest eyes shall cea-e to weep—
 " He giveth his beloved sleep! "

THE OUTCAST.

SHE GAZED at the pitiless sky,
 At the cold and barren earth,
At the hungry river rushing by,
And in deep dispair resolved to die,
 Cursing her hour of birth.
Her soul was deeply stained by crime—
A wreck cast up from the city's slime.

Why does she tremble and shrink
 At the ghastly thought of death?
Why does she fear Lethe's cup to drink?
Why fear in oblivion's arms to sink,
 If this life is but a breath?
Does the spirit-germ in her darkened soul
Revolt at death as man's final goal?

Does a vision of childhood hours
 Sweep o'er her fevered brain?
A dream of wildwood bowers,
Of sunshine, buds and flowers,
 Before temptation came?
A vision of home and its bliss, now lost
To her sin-sick soul so tempest-tossed?

The bell in the church-tower gray,
  Within whose shadow she stands,
Is calling believers to kneel and pray,
While the "gate of hell" just over the way
  Throws its red light across the sand
To where the river's cold, dark wave
The hem of her fouler garment laves.

"If I should kneel with the rest to pray,
  I wonder if God would hear?
I am weary of sin's unhallowed sway—
Will no one teach me the better way?"
  She cried in her doubt and fear;
But with glances of hate and insolent pride,
By the pious throng she was thrust aside.

We talk of "*this* gospel day!"
  We call *this* a Christian land!
Oh, God! when a sinner to Thee would pray,
From the temple's gate she is turned away
  Alone in the street to stand.
Wantonly, wickedly forced from the light,
Left fainting and dizzy in darkness and night.

And when, in the dreary morn,
  With white lips evermore dumb,
With garments ooze-dripping and torn,
With face hunger-stamped and sin-worn,
  She's dragged from the river's slum,
Can you, from your brow, wash the mark of Cain?
Can you call from earth's depths the soul you have slain?

THE ANGELS OF THE FLOWERS.

A SWEET May breeze from the South-land
   Whispered a wondrous tale,
And the sun, from his golden quiver,
   Sent arrows o'er hill and dale.

They pierced the mist of the morning,
   They scattered the chill of night,
And filled the earth with a glory
   That dazzled the angels' sight.

Then-Modesty called up her violets,
   Fragrant, and dewy, and fair;
And, hiding them under the green leaves,
   Watched them with tenderest care.

Purity scattered white lilies;
   Love brought her roses red;
Peace, with her wreath of laurel,
   Crowned the stern mountain's head.

Charity spread her green mosses,
   Over rocks dreary and brown;
While Faith, bending over the snow-drop,
   Wrought her a silvery crown.

Hope, with her apple-blooms fragrant,
   Gave promise of harvests to come;
While the blue-bird, among the gay branches,
   Was building his little thatch home.

But fairer than roses or lilies,
  Were the maidens who gathered the flowers,
Singing the beauties of May-day
  Under the leafy bowers.

And fairest of all the fair maidens
  Was Annie the queen of the day—
As she sat on a throne in the sunlight,
  Wreathed with the blossoms of May.

Alas, that Time's shadows should darken!
  Alas, that Death's powers should chill!
May-day they crowned her with roses,
  The next—every heart-beat was still!

May flowers still bloomed in the woodland,
  The sunlight lay fair on the hill,
But beauty of bud or of blossom
  No more her pure spirit can thrill.

No more? Faith whispers a story
  Of flowers that ne'er fade away;
Of rivers and cities of glory,
  And treasures that never decay.

Though pale as a bowed broken lily
  In her coffin they laid her away,
A far brighter crown she is wearing—
  Dear Annie, the queen of the May.

A LEGEND.

ROUND a ruined tower, cheerless and gray,
 The ivy clung;
In the belfry old, hung a rusty bell,
 With silent tongue,

And the trees stood round like friars grim,
While the mistletoe crept from limb to limb.

Around the garden there is a wall,
 The wall is steep;
Within the garden there is a well,
 ' The well is deep;
Around, above, the wild wind grieves,
And strews the ground with withered leaves.

No mortal in the moonlight pale,
 E'er lingers there;
Belated travelers hurry by
 With silent prayer;
For the legend says: "One dreary night,
In the lonely well, Truth hid from sight."

Mortals are more afraid of Truth
 Than sheeted ghost;
Their claims to love her honest face,
 An idle boast;
For the whole world scorns the honest poor,
And smiles on a villain with golden dower.

You ask me why the Truth should hide,
 Deep in the well?
Her friends are few, her foes great power

No man may tell!
When Falsehood's chariot rattles by,
Few know, or care, where Truth may lie.

Perhaps, when ages roll away
    And men grow wise,
God's Sun will light that garden chill,
    And Truth may rise;
Then, the serpents, Pride and Lust,
Their crested heads shall trail in dust.

THE CITY.

DESCRIBE the city! Ah, where begin?
With its palace-homes, or haunts of sin?
With its dingy dens, where the midnight lamp
Burns pale in the fetid cellar damp—
Burns pale, while age and childhood creep
Down slimy stairs from the dreary street.

Shall I tell of prisoners hidden, where
There comes no breath of heaven's pure air?
Of youth and beauty fallen low,
Of steps that ever downward go,
Till angels, weeping, turn aside
Where no plank bridges the loathsome tide?

Prisons and churches are builded high,
In their shadow the cringing thief shrinks by;
The blood-red light aluring shines
Where the tempter coils in the sparkling wines;
And the ceaseless "click" of ivory balls
On the gambler's ear like music falls.

Describe the city! A pen of fire,
In angel's hand that would never tire,
Would fail to paint the ghastly gloom
Of dark crime-haunted dens of doom,
Where rum-made maniacs—eyes aglare—
With oaths pollute the midnight air.

Some spend the night in dance and play,
Others by death-beds, kneeling, pray.
The murderer, with stealthy tread,
In darkness hides the dagger red;
And ever restless, weary feet
Wear to dust the stony street.

And must this fearful march of crime
Go ever on till the end of time?
Forever on in a chaos wild,
Souls sin-begotten and sin-defiled,
Sowing their seed of hate and woe,
Waiting and watching to see it grow?

O! for a love that would reach the hearts
Of the "Arabs" who throng the crowded marts;
For a voice to pierce the soul of those
Who deal out death and endless woes—
For power to whisper: "Peace, be still,"
To the surging tide of human ill.

Is God well pleased with offered gold
While the love he claims is waxing cold?
Alas, for people; alas, for priest!
Where are "Christ's poor" in your gospel feasts?
Have you whispered to lowly sinners: "Come
And find in the 'union' hope and home?"

In pride you have builded your temples high,
Reaching the blue of the arching sky.
Will fire on the gilded altar burn,
When heaven's commands you so lightly spurn?
When "forms" and fashion and vain display
In pulpit and pew hold ruthless sway?

Dare Christians talk of their mission bands,
Laboring in far and foreign lands,
While a worse than heathen darkness bides,
In haunts where crime its foulness hides,
And a darker than Burman darkness rests,
O'er the vaunted cities of the West? "

———

YOUTH AND AGE.

List' to the music o'er the way,
Children singing at their play:
"Around, around,
Our king is found,"
Keeping time as round they go,
Cheeks and eyes and lips a-glow.

A sad-eyed woman drawing near,
Half smiles, the quaint old song to hear:
"Around, around,
Our king is found."
Memory restores the sunny day,
Of happy childhood's careless play.

An old man bent with three score years,
In his dim eyes, feels gathering tears,
Pausing to hear,

The distich queer—
O! where are those who used to sing
When *he* stood in the whirling ring?

Alas! of all that happy throng,
He, only, found the journey long.
Full many a mound,
In sacred ground,
Guarded by marble, white and chill,
In few brief words the story tell.

Oh! there are " trifles, light as air,"
That seem to blot out years of care,
While memory pale,
Uplifts the vail,
And we behold the checkered way
Our feet have pressed since childhood's day.

If we have whispered words of cheer
To other weary travelers here:
Sincere in heart,
To do our part,
To help the brotherhood of man,
According to Christ's loving plan;

If we have loved truth's holy ways—
If we, by faith, can heavenward gaze,
We'll say good-bye,
To years that lie
Like milestones 'long the backward way,
Nor long for childhood's sunny day.

THY WAY.

On TIME's solemn shores I am standing,
  Fair Hope has taken her flight,
The flowers in Love's garden have faded
  And perished, in Pain's bitter night.

My path is by Death over-shadowed,
  Love's hand-clasp is broken in twain,
From the realms of the dead, for one whisper,
  Heart-sick I have listened in vain.

My day draws near to its closing,
  The sands in the glass running low--
And over life's hill-slope the twilight
  Grows purple, in night's afterglow.

"No night!" where the loved one is straying,
  No parting, no sorrow, no tears!
No shadow in all the bright mornings
  That make up eternity's years!

O, Savior! in doubt and in darkness,
  In the hours of my weakness and pain,
Let me hold to thy dear hand, believing
  Earth's sorrows are never in vain!

Let me follow thy feet in the desert,
  Thy way through the valley of tears,
Thy path up the steeps of the mountain—
  Thy love over-arching all fears.

Speak to my soul 'mid the shadows,
  From my pathway all sunshine has fled;
As I pass through the gloom of the midnight
  Let faith light the stars overhead.

A PRAYER.

O, Savior, watch this night with me!
  I dare not watch alone!
For pain's dark presence veils God's face
  And hides the heavenly home!
And faith grows weak, and prayers seem vain,
  The way I can not see,
The cross is heavy and I faint;
  Dear Savior, strengthen me!

In my sad heart's Gethsemane,
  To thee alone I cry,
For withered leaves, and faded flowers,
  Along my pathway lie—
The sport of every idle wind,
  Their beauty long since fled,
And voices of the past wail out
  A requiem of the dead.

Toll, funeral bells! toll for dead hopes,
  For joys too sweet to last,
For sunny skies, which gathering clouds
  Too quickly overcast!

Dreams of ambition, dreams of love,
    All frail and earth-born things,
For to them all, since mortals sinned,
    The curse of Eden clings.

Dear Jesus, I would walk with thee!
    I can not walk alone—
The earthly path that I must tread,
    With thorns is over-grown!
The clouds are thick above my head,
    I can not see the light,
But with Thy true hand leading me,
    I will not fear the night.

WISHES.

ADDRESSED TO MRS. A. R. BENTON.

IF I WERE the brightest star in heaven,
    That burns on the brow of night,
My fairest beam should fall on thee,
    And make thy pathway bright.

If I were the fairest of roses fair,
    I would give my sweetest breath,
Glad, in dying, if thy pure lips
    Caressed me e'en in death.

If I were a "charm" no darkling pain,
    Should dim thy brightest hour;
Balm, on the breeze of morn should come,
    With its breath of healing power.

If I were a gem, in ocean's cave,
  I would plead with the restless sea,
That from the voiceless, trackless depths,
  I should be "wave tossed" to thee.

If I were the soul of music sweet,
  I would sing thee a song divine,
I would soothe thy soul with fairy strains
  Pure from the spirit's shrine.

If I were the spirit of hope,
  I would weave a spell so fair,
That thy path should ever be as blessed,
  As "the paths of angels are. '

I think, were angels thy face to see,
  To heaven they would quickly fly
To ask if a spirit, glory crowned,
  Had wandered from the sky.

'TIS HOME WHERE THE HEART IS.

"WHERE is thy home?" I asked a laughing boy
  Who, gladly whistling, roamed the breezy hills;
His face lit up with looks of artless joy:
  "My home? 'tis where my own dear mother dwells!"

"Where is thy home?" I asked a maiden fair
  Who watched her lover join the warrior band;
"My home," she cried, "is where young Roderick roams
  Upon his milk-white charger—in a distant land."

"Where is thy home?" I asked a yeoman strong,
　　Who swung his scythe to merry roundelay:
"'Tis where my children and their mother dwell;
　　Yon cot, o'er which the sweet, wild roses stray."

"Where is thy home? O, aged Christian, where,
　　Amid the strife and toil of weary years?"
"My home? not on the rocky shores of time,
　　But, where the jasper walls and golden gates appear."

THE WOODLAND RIVER.

I WANDERED in the shadowy wood,
　　When April, fair and wise,
Kissed the arbutus' dewy lips
　　Till she blushed in shy surprise.
A dreaming fountain lay asleep,
　　With a lily on her breast,
While sheeny willows, bending low,
　　Guarded her place of rest.

"O, happy fountain, hid secure
　　Through time's unnumbered years,
Would, I thus slept in nature's arms,
　　Secure from life's dark tears."
I paused, the fountain's silver voice
　　Murmured this solemn thought:
"To labor is the better creed;
　　By pain all peace is bought."

I wandered on, a tiny brook
   Dancing, joyous and free,
Carried unbought beauty and life
   To fern, and flower, and tree.
But ah, the little hill-side stream
   Grew broad, and deep, and grand,
And sweeping down the jagged rocks,
   Its thunders shook the land.

For lo, earth's rocky fingers failed
   To hold the waters rife;
Dashing the white spray from their brow,
   They shout: "Labor is life."
And thus, O, valley-stream, I learn
   God's promises abound,
With earnest of a perfect rest
   To man, when labor-crowned.

THE YEAR'S DIARY.

THE SOUTH wind whispers, and from the mold
The thousand beauties of spring unfold—
Blue-eyed violets, daisies fair,
Wild sweet-brier and maiden-hair.

The plow-boy, whistling, mocks the quail,
And the children launch their tiny sail
In the meadow brook, that bears away
The mimic ship to the distant bay.

Like a dream of hope, the spring-time fades,
And mazy summer fills the glades;

The cricket croons his drowsy note,
The butterfly plumes his gorgeous coat.

Amid the aisles of growing corn,
The poppy smiles to the smiling morn,
And the gladsome lark sings a roundelay
Amid the swathes of new-mown hay.

Wild and exultant, merry and glad,
But never a note complaining or sad;
And the farmer sighs, as he catches the air,
"If I, like the lark, were but free from care."

Then he turned his steps where the meadow hay,
Fresh in its dewy sweetness lay,
And murmured the while: "The set of sun
Will find me still with my task undone."

But summer ended, the harvest was o'er,
The reaper had gathered his golden store;
The song of the cricket is hushed and still,
And brown leaves shiver in winds a-chill.

"Autumn is dying," the north wind sighs;
"Autumn is dying," the cold earth cries;
And *my* heart is filled with a sad unrest,
For hopes have faded—I loved the best.

Farewell! Old Year; you have digged a grave
For the love of one I'd have died to save;
How, then, can I make a New Year's feast?
And who shall I bid as a New Year's guest?

Hope is dead! but Faith shall be
The guest that I bid to sup with me.

God sends her—lest I go astray;
In all coming days she shall lead the way.

God giveth us all another year,
To sow our seed, in his holy fear.
Farewell! Old Year; duty's the goal
That henceforth shall gleam before my soul.

Though weary and rough the mountain's track,
My eyes to the plain shall ne'er turn back;
But I'll pray for strength for the weary way,
Which is ushered in on this New Year's day.

THE CHRISTIAN POETESS, MARIE R. BUTLER.

SHE dwells upon a holy mount,
 From mortals set apart,
And drinks from that celestial fount,
 Which purifies the heart;
She joys the heavenly seed to sow,
Which in God's field shall thrive and grow.

The angels kissed her as she slept,
 Her lips were sanctified;
They o'er her heart their vigils kept
 Till song was glorified;
Like dews of Hermon o'er her head,
The gifts that angels bring were shed.

No vain, no idle song she sings,
 Priestess to poesy's shrine,
The bright, pure fancies that she brings,

God's Spirit makes divine.
Her words, like manna, fall to bless
The wanderers in life's wilderness.

The loathsome serpents, pride and sin,
    That trail beneath the leaves,
From her pure pen no tolerance win—
    She binds no mildewed sheaves;
Yet her broad, loving charity
Is deep and boundless as the sea.

She sings of Christ, our thorn-crowned King,
    Who bowed to God's behest,
And gathered all death's bitter pangs
    To his own sinless breast.
The tones that thrill earth's purple skies,
But echo Heaven's grand harmonies.

———

POOR FARMER JOHN.

OLD FARMER John is sore perplexed—
Nay, farmer John is really vexed:
He labors early, labors late,
Yet ever talks of adverse fate;
For all his toilings scarce suffice,
Of longed-for lands to pay the price.

The summers come, the summers go,
The spring showers waste the winter's snow
The while, from dawn till close of day,

Receiving naught but frowns for pay;
His good wife toils, and anxious care
Has faded lip and cheek and hair.

Acres on acres stretch away
Of woodland, corn, of wheat and hay;
His cattle roam o'er many a hill,
His brooklet turns the groaning mill;
Yet still he sighs and longs for more,
And grumbles e'er that he is poor.

Four sturdy sons, four daughters fair
Claim at his hands a father's care.
He gave them labor without end,
And strove their souls, like his, to bend
Into the narrow groove of thought:
"Gold to be earned, land to be bought."

Yes, farmer John is growing poor!
You feel it as you pass his door.
His old brown house is small and mean,
The roof is warped by crack and seam;
The leaning bars, the half-hinged door,
Proclaim old John is *very* poor.

No books: no pictures on the wall;
Carpetless rooms and dreary hall.
Why think it strange such farmers' boys
Should seek the city's pomp and noise?
Should learn to loathe the sight of home,
Where naught of joy or grace may come?

Why think it strange his poor, old wife,
Who coined for him her very life,
Should pause at last, despite his frown,

And lay her weary burden down
In joy, to walk the streets of heaven?
Where naught is sold, but all is given?

Go where you will, search earth around,
The poorest man that can be found,
Is he who toils, through life, to gain
Widest extent of hill and plain;
Forgetting all his soul s best needs,
In counting o'er his title-deeds.

———

SUBMISSION.

"THY WILL be done!" thus we are taught to pray
            By lips divine.
"Thy will be done!" Ah, can we always say
            "Thy will," not mine?
   'Mid tears and loss and pain,
   When all the past seems vain,
   And death the greatest gain,
   Can we still say: "Thy will, thine alway?"

"Thy will be done," with Thee I would abide.
            Cease, burning tears!
"Thy will be done!" Perish, O, heart of pride
            And earth-born fears!
   Soul, still thy frantic cries
   O'er broken human ties;
   Though hope in anguish dies
   A wiser will than man's, shall be my guide.

"Thy will be done!" I whisper, bending low,
 "Thy will, not mine!"
When waves of pain, my sad soul overflow,
 The Hand divine
Can shield from sorrow's dart—
Can heal the wounded heart
From loved ones doomed to part:
Thy will, Thine only would I know.

GOD'S PROMISE.

WHILE Autumn mourns her falling leaves,
And God calls for his ripened sheaves;
While storms are beating on my head,
And every joy of earth is dead,
Faith whispers: "This is promised thee:
'As is thy day, thy strength shall be.'"

The earth mourns a lost ray of light,
But radiant spheres have grown more bright,
The key of Faith has opened wide
The star-locked gate across the tide;
And comes from thence this melody:
"As is thy day, thy strength shall be."

"There is no day without its night:"
No hope but feels sorrow's dread blight.
To Death's cold sceptre hearts must bow,

And withered leaves crown every brow;
But still God's promise comes to me:
"As is thy day, thy strength shall be."

When fevered heart-beats waste the life,
And all the air with pain is rife:
When all the earth can yield no rest,
And anguish 'bides within my breast,
Comes answer to my agony:
"As is thy day, thy strength shall be."

Ah! those who up the mountain climb
With bleeding feet, to heights sublime;
Who reach the home beyond the stars,
Whisper back, through golden bars:
"Receive God's promise trustingly:
'As is thy day, thy strength shall be.'"

Aged and helpless! O, my soul!
Before thee is the promised goal,
And God-commissioned Death draws near
To hush all heart-ache.   Dost thou fear?
The midnight stars whisper to thee:
"As is thy day, thy strength shall be."

DOES HE KNOW ?

Does He know the weary way?
The clouds that overcast the day?
The thorns that pierce me when I stray?

Does He know how hard the fight?
The fears which the lone heart afright?
The darkness of the starless night?

Does He know, when sad and lorn,
When lost each earthly hope, we mourn,
Our hearts by fearful conflict torn?

Does He know, how fierce and wild
The tempest beats upon His child,
Out-reaching for climes undefiled?

Does He know the toil and care?
The longing cries, the ceaseless prayer ?
For strength to do and strength to bear?

As Hagar found, when in her flight
Abra'am's white tents faded from sight,
Her darkest hour o'er-crowned with light,

When wandering in our desert drear,
Bowed down with anguish, doubt and fear,
Shall we too find our angel near?

Will He our load of weary care
Lift from our hearts, and kindly bear
Whene'er we light the lamp of prayer?

When wrecked upon life's raging sea,
Tossed upon breakers "on the lee,"
Will He the life-boat send to me?

Weak and trembling with afright,
How can I sail where all is night?
How can I find the beacon light?

Or will He whisper, soft and low,
"*Peace*," when winds too fiercely blow?
When o'er me deepest waters flow?

Will He bid the waves recede
In the soul's hour of darkest need,
Nor "break the bruised and bending reed?"

When we can say: "Thy will be done!"
We then can know the battle won,
And peace of heaven on earth begun.

By patient doing, glory's won!
By swift hours flitting, life is done!
By faith's hand-clasping, heaven's begun!

HIDDEN LIFE.

Plant the seed in the silent earth,
The Master will give it a glorious birth;
Mysterious life's in the casket brown—
A royal robe and a golden crown.

And soon from its lowly grave 'twill rise,
A gift from the garden of Paradise,

With lips dew-laden, wondrous fair,
A child of the sun, a bride of the air.

Are ye weary, toiling from morn till night?
A blessing will follow, but *do* the right;
There is no harvest for idle hands,
No grapes where thistle or brier stands.

No lilies, white as the drifting snow,
In bramble thickets will bud and blow.
The lowly pansy, with violet eyes,
Neglected, weeps, and weeping dies.

Life's dreariest spot may yield sweet flowers,
And its darkest day have some sunny hours;
But only the toilers will see the sun,
Or gather the flowers when the day is done.

There's a promise on every hill-side brown,
When Autumn shall shower her blessings down;
Then plant the seed and prune the vine,
For the harvest is sure, in God's good time.

OUR LIFE DREAM.

How OFTEN they tell us 'tis only a dream—
  This beautiful life of ours—
That, floating with hope down the amber-waved stream,
  In her shallop, 'mid fairy-like flowers,
We shall wake by-and-by on a tempest-tossed sea,
  And our bark will be shattered and torn;

The flower-banked river lie far at our lee,
 While our white sails are drooping and lorn.

Life is not a dream—the waves may be wild,
 And its waters well nigh overwhelm—
The tempest of old obeyed the voice mild,
 While Faith, with her hand on the helm,
Steered through the black midnight of old Galilee;
 So we, with *one Star* for our guide,
Shall conquer the sorrows of life's stormy sea,
 And its dangers and tempests outride.

A HOME ON THE OTHER SIDE.

I HAD launched my boat on a stormy sea,
 The waves were rolling high;
The roar of the breakers met my ear—
 And dark clouds met my eye!

Pain was the pilot that steered the bark,
 Over the ocean of tears,
And I heard him laugh a horrible laugh,
 As he spoke of the coming years.

We are steering now for the river of death,
 He said in terrible glee,
And the demons joined their mocking laugh,
 With the roar of the angry sea.

Faster and faster the boat sailed on;
 Near was the rushing tide

That severs the world from the great unknown,
  Which lies on the other side.

I cried in my agonizing grief;
  I prayed for strength and aid;
A Star arose in the distant East,
  And its beams on the waters played.

I am sailing still towards the river of death,
  But Bethlehem's Star is my guide
To a life of duty—a peaceful death,
  And a home on the other side.

A TRIBUTE OF LOVE.

ADDRESSED TO MRS. S. J. PEARCE.

ON EARTH thou bearest a sacred name,
And angels to thee kindred claim,
    And guard thy onward road.
The sick, the weary and oppressed,
Find in thy presence peace and rest;
And nightly prayers for thee ascend,
From those who love and call thee friend,
    Remembering thee to God.

Thou art enshrined by truth and love;
And bounteous blessings from above
    Are scattered round thy way.
A type of heaven thy dwelling place,
An angel-beauty in thy face,

So soul-illumined; and thine eye
Has caught a glory from on high,
 To light life's changeful day.

From the pure altar of thy home,
Thy loved ones never long to roam,
 'Mid life's temptations dark;
For over all its lambent skies
Thou art the sun that glorifies—
The sweet o'er-mastering influence still,
To win from every thought of ill,
 The dove of thy dear ark.

A sacred heritage from heaven,
Thy noble mind to thee was given,
 A lamp to bless and guide
Those who in bondage sigh and moan,
Those who in darkness walk alone;
Thy charity broad as the skies,
Kindles a flame that never dies,
 O'er-reaching death's cold tide.

Thou'st long since reached faith's mountain height,
And standing there, in God's pure light,
 Heaven is not far from thee;
And sweet Hope whispers: " Yonder blue
But hides **the** glorified from view—
The household band—behold they wait
For thee beside the star-gemmed gate,
 'Near to the Jasper sea.' "

DEAD?

You CALL him dead?   He has gone before,
And, waiting, stands by the open door,
With a star on his brow to light my way,
Lest, the path grown dark, my feet should stray.

"His voice is silent?"   Ah, no! a prayer
Is borne to my ears on the midnight air:
"She is lonely now in a weary land;
Guard her, dear Lord, that her feet may stand,

Firm on the Rock! "   Ah! light and life
Must e'er be born of clouds and strife;
And the blood-stained cross of Palestine,
Saw the Son of Man crowned Lord Divine.

When mists arise like phantoms gray,
Faith parts the veil of doubt and fear,
And we see the "Glory of the Lord"
Shine softly out through the midnight drear.

Grief's ministry, fast-falling tears,
Must overshadow the coming years;
While all is darkness, above, around,
I know God loveth the sorrow-crowned.

SPIRIT LONGINGS.

Eternity's watchers! bright gleaming stars!
 O, make me a ladder of light,
That from these low valleys of sorrow and weeping,
 I may climb to your infinite height!

O, angels of glory! throw open your doors,
 Your wondrous songs would I hear,
As they float down through ether, from regions elysian,
 Where dwelleth no shadow or fear!

Spirit of Beauty! in letters of light,
 We read of the "glory to be,"
On golden-crowned mountains, flower-wreathed valleys
 And the unwritten songs of the sea.

O, Night! let me hide in your mantle's dark folds,
 For, haply, to loved ones once more,
The feet of the ransomed, through pearl-gates may wander
 Back from eternity's shore!

Rainbow of Promise! o'er hilltops of gold,
 Let my feet, from these lowlands of pain,
Cross over your bars of purple and azure,
 To the fount on the evergreen plain!

 Dreams of the night time! O, whisper to me,
 Of the rapturous joy of that home,
Where, deathless, they dwell in mansions of glory,
 Who from earth's pathways have gone!

Winds of the morning! O, bear me away,
  For, see the pearl-gates half unfold,
While I kneel in the dawn, and gaze through the portal
  On the loved ones now safe in the fold!

Voice of the Past! only tears canst thou give,
  And regrets for the day that is done!
But thy skeleton fingers! O, Time, are still pointing
  To battle-fields yet to be won!

THE WOMAN'S WAR.

"A war to be remembered"
  Falls from a poet's pen
Remembered! Yes! while ages
  Roll o'er the works of men.

"Down with the tyrant Alcohol!"
  And legions of the strong,
Brave women of the nation rise
  And fill the air with song.

They sing of the Redeemer,
  And with a faith divine
They brave the stormy elements
  And form in battle line.

With singing and with prayers
  They meet Satanic hosts

Though slandered, stoned, imprisoned,
　Their faith is never lost.

Wielding no carnal weapons,
　Theirs is a bloodless fight,
Yet a New Age and better day
　Is ushered into light.

In patience, never weary
　With power before unknown;
The "Spirit Sword" they're wielding,
　Wrong will be overthrown.

The very earth is startled,
　At the rays of light, sublime,
Which are lighting up the glory,
　On the brow of coming time.

Deliverance, lo! it cometh!
　Prayer is never breathed in vain—
Never wasted—God who hears it,
　Sends in answer "growth and gain."

Pray on, "Daughters of Heaven!"
　In all the coming time,
The echoing arch of centuries,
　Shall "hold your lives sublime."

PALMYRA.

"City of Palms!" alone, alone
    Amid the arid sand,
Peopleless wreck of ages past,
    Thy broken columns stand,
Thy haughty pride to earth is crushed,
Thy crowded marts to silence hushed.
    The wild beast of the desert roams
    , Through sacred halls 'neath ruined domes;
Silence and mystery entomb
Thy fabled courts, thy gardens' bloom.

O, fallen Queen! O, desert Star!
    Thy light is dimmed and gone,
And darkness rests o'er Syrian plains
    Where once thy glory shone.
The moaning wind, the jackal's cry,
The wandering Arab passing by,
    The palsied pulse, the phantom tread
    Are signets of a city dead,
A mighty tomb, a ghastly sleep,
A wreck, which earth's dim records keep.

Dark night "sits brooding o'er decay,"
    Girt 'round by voiceless space,
While the deep mystery of death
    Enfolds a vanished race.
From Roman lips the mandate came;
The sword flashed like a breath of flame;

Zenobia's doom and thine were sealed,
 Upon the midnight battle-field,
And the proud car of Roman state,
For all time left thee desolate.

Deserted fane and battlement!
 War-broken shaft and tower!
In thee we see earth's littleness,
 The end of pride and power.
While drifting sands entomb their prey,
Hiding from man they slow decay,
 Where only funeral ivy twines
 'Round rifled tombs and ruined shrines;
Life's storied pages can but seem
Pale meteor lights on Time's swift stream.

FAITH.

ARE YOU often sad and weary?
Do life's paths seem dark and dreary?
Cease all sinning, cease all grieving,
Jesus calls, O, come believing!

Mourner, sad and broken hearted,
From thy loved ones art thou parted?
Hark! a voice to thee is crying,
" Look aloft, " and cease all sighing.

See, the heavy cross is glorious,
Since the bleeding Lamb victorious

Conquered death and sin and sorrow,
Lifting clouds from Death's to-morrow.

Have you faith? then never falter,
Lay your heart upon God's altar,
For however weary, weeping,
Jesus holds thee in His keeping.

Have you faith! in City glorious,
Christ the Loving's gone before us,
For the faithful, pure and lowly,
Builds a mansion fair and holy.

Faith's the password into Heaven,
When love has all our sins forgiven,
Where beside life's glittering river
Faith is lost in sight forever.

HOME.

You TELL me the little cottage stands
  'Neath the same wide spreading trees;
That vines o'er-clamber the rustic porch,
  And imprison the summer breeze.
No longer to us is it " Home, sweet home; "
  For sunshine, nor fairest flowers,
Can bring to our hearts the love and hope,
  Or joy, of the vanished hours.

Hours which memory alone holds fast,
　　Safe from unhallowed hands,
As the ocean holds her purest gems
　　Enwrapped in her silver sands.
On mount or plain, o'er all the earth,
　　Home can never more be found;
Silent, we bow our heads in dust,
　　And in tears are sorrow-crowned.

Home! 'tis alone where a mother's hands
　　Shut the door on grief and tears,
Where the mystic gate of love is locked
　　'Gainst care and earth-born fears.
Alas! a grave its shadow casts,
　　Heavy and dark, and cold
Across the hearth where hope had strewn
　　Joy-buds that can ne'er unfold.

Do souls straightway forget the cross,
　　As they gaze on the glorified One?
Or do they look back o'er the blood-tracked path,
　　And watch how our battles are won?
Does the dazzling light of eternal day
　　From their gaze shut our tear-stained eyes?
Do the songs of the blessed so thrill their hearts
　　That they hear not our anguished cries?

If the pearly gates, by angel guards,
　　For a moment unclosed might be,
Could we catch the song our loved ones sing
　　To-day by the Jasper sea,
The path that our faltering feet must tread,
　　As we're " passing under the rod,"
Would seem less drear could we hear the songs
　　They sing in the " city of God."

LIFE'S LESSON.

The tiny seed, in the furrow deep,
  Buried in darkness and wet with rain,
Waking to life from its silent sleep,
  Holdeth its life-work not in vain.
And not in vain is the gloom of night,
Since from out the darkness springeth the light,
Since from out the death-mold, the growing corn
So glorified, waiteth the harvest morn.

The flower that blooms in the forest aisles,
  Afar from the ken of human sight,
Looks to the skies and lovingly smiles,
  Upward reaching to life and light;
Glad in that life, since the Father who made,
Shelters her there in the mossy-green glade.
Ah! not in vain, since He willeth it so
Do the shy wild flowers in their beauty grow.

The brook, half hidden by ferny banks,
  Sings gladsome songs of sweet content,
And the stately pines in serried ranks,
  And hardy laurels, gnarled and bent,
Ne'er murmur when storm-clouds are hov'ring nigh,
Or tempests, black-winged, sweep over the sky;
But with upraised arms, they evermore pray:
"Give us strength, dear Lord, for the darkest day."

The endelwisse, on the Alpine height,
  Amid the glaciers lifts its face,
Pure as a dream, in the glowing light,
  Child of the snowy mountain place;

Alone in the storm she veileth her eyes,
Shy, pale and sweet, 'neath the snow-laden skies,
Glad since the Father hath made her so fair,
The trials he sends to lovingly bear.

The storm-cleft rock where the lichen creeps,
    Growing gray in the march of time,
Of long past ages a record keeps;
    Nations may fall, yet still, sublime,
Shall the age-worn turrets unshaken stand,
To teach us the power of the Master's hand;
That hand oft chastens, yet, afar, through the gloom,
On the dark rough rock, see the roses bloom.

Then garner for aye, lessons of hope;
    Cling to your faith in sorrow's night;
Trim your ship's sails! hold fast to the rope!
    After darkness cometh the light.
Learn then from nature that no life is vain,
Though shadowed by darkness, sorrow and pain;
This lesson is taught, with each passing hour,
That *strengthened by duty, weakness is power.*

HERE AND HEREAFTER.

O 'TIS the saddest thing, to bear
    A saddened heart,
To know, that in the busy world
    I have no part;

To know that other hands must sow,
    And others reap;
To know that I can never climb
    The mountain steep;

That on its top I may not stand
    In sunlight free;
That only barren, storm-swept heaths
    Remain for me.

The past is rife with haunting dreams,
    Dreams that have fled—
Spectres dark from shadow-land,
    Hopes that are dead.

*   *   *   *   *

Ah! 'tis the gladdest thing to know,
    While here I weep,
That when the weary day is done,
    Comes rest and sleep;

That while I walk life's tangled path
    With bleeding feet—
Where flowers by thorns are overgrown—
    'Mid summer's heat,

That Beulah's green and shady groves
 Are just in sight,
Where storms and darkness may not come,
 And all is light.

The passing years may come and go,
 The rains may fall—
But love, that only wounds to heal,
 Is over all.

The clouds may darken all my skies,
 And life may fail;
But only light and love are found
 Beyond the veil.

THE OCEAN-DEAD.

The ocean's restless, never ceasing moan—
 The music of the "ever sounding sea"—
A mystic song to all the ages past,
 A mystic song in ages yet to be.

Ah! do they sing of those who sweetly rest
 Amid bright shells and golden-gleaming sands,
Who through the death-cold waters, dark and deep,
 Triumphant passed to reach the glory-land?

The blue waves sweep above the forms of kings;
 Right royal is the shroud their loom er-weaves,
Of emeralds, amber, amethyst, and gold,
 In hues as rare as autumn's richest leaves.

Youth and old age together fell asleep,
  All dreamlessly, upon a bed of pearls;
Bright gems entwine the scattered locks of gray,
  And form a wreath for childhood's silken curls.

Pearl-lighted halls beneath the crested waves,
  Weary earth-feet may never, never tread;
Nor earthly voice e'er break the silence deep,
  Which icily enwraps the ocean-dead.

The saddest soul may find a sweet repose—
  A painless sleep, within the ocean's breast,
Where galling chains, which wearily are worn,
  At last are loosed, leaving an endless rest.

Ah, blessed sleep! sleep of the ocean-dead!
  No weary earth-moan wakes their last repose;
For them the grand memorial shall be
  Chanted, till angel hands Time's Book shall close.

AUTUMNALIS.

Hopes that have faded away, like the leaves,
  And buds of promise unblown,
The trailing arbutus, and hemlock and rue,
  Have been woven into my crown.
Since a crown of thorns the Master wore,
Shall I grieve that roses are not my store?

I know that my wreath of pale "Autumn Leaves,"
  Is faded, withered and brown,
But humbly, now, at the foot of the cross,
  I will lay my offering down;
Mayhap, the Master, who knoweth all pain,
Will whisper: "Your toiling is not in vain."

www.ingramcontent.com/pod-product-compliance
Lightning Source LLC
Chambersburg PA
CBHW031115020726
47495CB00007B/2203